W9-CBQ-987

Henry Alford has written for numerous publications, including *Details, The New York Observer, Spy, Vanity Fair, Vogue, Washington Monthly,* and *The New York Times*. He has also appeared on *The Tonight Show* with Jay Leno and *Late Night* with Conan O'Brien. He lives in New York City.

MUNICIPAL BONDAGE

Henry Alford

RIVERHEAD BOOKS, NEW YORK

Riverhead Books
Published by The Berkley Publishing Group
200 Madison Avenue
New York, NY 10016

Cover design by James R. Harris
Cover author photo by Jill Levine
Cover background photo by Index Stock Photography

Random House hardcover ISBN: 0–679–41509–2
First Riverhead edition: September 1995
Riverhead ISBN: 1–57322–510–X

Published simultaneously in Canada.

Library of Congress Cataloging-in-Publication Data

Alford, Henry, 1962-
    Municipal bondage / Henry Alford. — 1st Riverhead ed.
        p.   cm.
    Originally published: 1st ed. New York : Random House, c1993.
    "Portions of this work were originally published, in different
form, in *Mademoiselle*, the *New York Observer, Spy,* and *Vogue*"—T.p.
verso.
    ISBN 1-57322-510-X (pbk.)
    1. American wit and humor.   I.   Title.
[PN6162.A365   1995]
814'.54—dc20   95-1678
                                                                          CIP

Printed in the United States of America.

10   9   8   7   6   5   4   3   2   1

For Jess and Mom

Contents

Lifestyling

Moving On

What Is Owed

When asked by my publisher to supply this book's reading line—a reading line being the explanatory phrase that comes between a book's title and its author's name, such as "A Novel" or "A Long, Dreary History of Shoe Manufacturing in Wales by"—I submitted the accurate and quite charming "Comic Investigations and Essays." However, as the observant reader will note, it lost out to "One Man's Anxiety-Producing Adventures in the Big City"—a concession to said publisher, who felt that prospective book buyers would take one look at the phrase *comic investigations* and become instantly addled and confused in the manner of a country store clerk who has lost his spectacles in the barley.

So I would ask you to be slightly indulgent on the reading-line front. After all, not everything contained herein is anxiety-producing; the selections are not all adventures—some are essays, some are lists, and one of the selections takes place on the not-so-big-city-riddled island of Jamaica. (But these quibbles aside, let me simply say that I think this whole "One Man's" business is *brilliant.*)

I broach this topic because there is some confusion about what I do. People unfamiliar with my work have, in the past, asked me how my "skits" are progressing. Having been told that I once went to Christie's auction house and asked two employees there to appraise my bizarre, spurious heirlooms; having gleaned that I once took a cocker spaniel to the Holiday Inn at the Newark airport, where I groomed him unconventionally in an attempt to pass the National Dog Groomers Association of America's certification test, these people proceed to refer to my undertakings as "skits."

But I beg to differ. Skits, as we all know, involve a funny doorbell, bad Southern accents, and actor Harvey Korman. *Pranks, capers, monkeyshines*—call the more activity-based portions of this book what you will. But do not call them *skits*. (And if you call me a *jackanape*, I will slap you.)

I suppose I prefer to think of my contribution to the history of letters as taking the form of "investigations" because the term alludes to that aspect of my work that takes the form of investigative journalism. In almost every case, the people with whom I interact in this book did not know, at the time of interaction, that I was preparing to write about them. Posing as an individual devoid of ulterior motive, I entered these peoples' lives and allowed my innocent mien and neurotic stammerings to put them off guard.

That there is something manipulative and unsavory about this journalistic method I will not dispute; in deference to this, I have tried to write about others' professional, as opposed to private, behavior. In some instances, however, the professional/personal line is blurred, and discretion is forced to take a backseat to journalistic vigor. Thus you will behold the clutter consultant who visited my apartment telling me about her imaginary friend, Claire; or the students at the Wilfred Beauty Academy—although they are expressly asked not to—warming up their lunches in the Academy's wig dryer.

Such disclosures may strike you as unseemly. Moreover, you may find that *my own* behavior as chronicled in this book exhibits a more-than-occasional lack of decorum. If such is the case, I would again ask for your indulgence; in vowing to push the envelope of the world around me, I have been given a compelling reason to vent many of my more unattractive personal habits.

For the record: I take responsibility for my actions; the views expressed herein—to the extent that there are views expressed herein—are my own. What I present as fact is, indeed, fact.

However, all this is not to say that the contents of this book are entirely of my own devising. No, no—mine is a life fairly teeming with little elves.

The Little Elves in My Life: An Appreciation

I would like to thank Random House's justly esteemed Jonathan Karp, who, after hearing me read at the Writer's Voice series several springs ago, wrote the letter of inquiry that set this book in motion. Unfortunately, this letter of inquiry spelled my name A-F-F-O-R-D—a harbinger of later contractual unzealousness—however, I applaud my editor's uncanny eye for the proverbial diamond in the rough.

I bring homage to Susan Morrison, who, over the years, has proffered much encouragement and many assignments. A careful reader, a generous colleague, an individual sensitive to the subtle tensions at the intersection of syntax and word choice—a woman, in short, with many, many synonyms for *nuance.*

Writing this book required me to spend many hours sequestered within my apartment. I offer apology to those friends whose invitations I have rebuffed during the past year, fearful that the overexposure to nightlife might taint the winsome quality of my prose.

From my speeding roadster of journalistic ambition, I obsequiously tip my hat to Kurt Andersen and Graydon Carter, men of influence and suspenders.

I thank David Handelman, who assessed my raw talent and uttered the lustrous words "male model."

I thank those editors at glamorous magazines—Misses Bell, Caruso, Doppelt, and Keller, and Misters Kamp and Tyrnauer—who have helped me to slowly drain the profit margin of the Condé Nast empire.

Literary agent Laura Blake, prose stylist Jim Collins, Christie's guide Seth Flicker, mother figure Joanne Gruber, Bergdorf's shopper Michael Hainey, nubbins flack George Kalogerakis, foreign-lover enthusiast Richard Kaye, Zsa Zsa–channeler Bob Mack, poetry angel Jamie Malanowski, Democratic Convention driver Erica Marcus, food goddess Francine Maroukian, animal handler Jane McQueen-

Mason, unwitting investor Jane Redmond, snack-food consultant Ann Shayne, and attractive personal assistant Jess Taylor: You are *all* my children.

And, lest I overlook any names in this dizzy-making festival of cross-promotion, lest I fail to mention any single living person who might be in a position to further my station in life, I invoke two final entities.

I mention Michael Ovitz. And I mention God.

MUNICIPAL
BONDAGE

HOMESTEADING

Please Please Me

It is the curse of the single person to be a perpetual witness to the splendors and privileges of matrimony. And among the amenities matrimony lavishes upon its participants, perhaps most galling is marriage's institutionalization of gift-giving. I think of bridal-shower gifts, I think of wedding gifts, I think of anniversary gifts; I think and then I shudder. For, although I do not begrudge a happy pair the perquisites of union, there was a time when I could not help but feel that my own grim existence—an existence devoted largely to going home each night, putting on some plaintive honky-tonk music and then dancing with a mop—was the very type that would most benefit from an influx of bright and shiny objects. My married friends had both each other *and* a drawerful of sterling asparagus prongs, I thought. I had my work.

Oh, certainly, when at Christmastime family members

handed me a new appliance or a biography of Saint Ignatius of Loyola, they partly assuaged this feeling of deprivation.

But the effect was short-lived.

So it was with joyous excitement that I learned about a program within Bloomingdale's bridal registry wherein single people can register for gifts even if they are not getting married. Although self-registry is usually done by people who are moving into a new apartment, I decided that there was no reason why someone in my position shouldn't pick out merchandise simply because, as I would later tell salespeople, "I like to receive and unwrap presents."

I'm not particularly devoted to the Bloomingdale's style, so I checked to see if other stores had similar consolation-prize autoregistry programs. Employees at Saks Fifth Avenue and Alexander's told me that their stores had neither bridal nor self registries; a somewhat harried older woman at Lord and Taylor told me that her store had discontinued its registry but that it did have a personal shopper who would walk around the store with customers and help them pick out things to buy.

"And then could I have other people buy them for me?" I asked.

"No, these are things that *you* would buy," she said.

"Oh," I said. "So there's no one here whom I can tell what merchandise I'm interested in having other people buy for me?"

"No," she said, her face starting to drain of all expression.

"Could I tell *you* what merchandise I'm interested in having other people buy me?"

"No."

Chastened, I moved on. A saleswoman in Macy's bridal registry allowed me to register but seemed uncertain about the process. When I asked her if I should put my name in the space on the form marked GROOM or the one marked BRIDE, she stared at me as if her mind had suddenly and unexpectedly been transported to some very distant location. This prompted the woman who was standing behind me to suggest, "Why not put your name in both, like you're marrying yourself"—a comment discomfitting in the keenness of its perception. So I followed the woman's advice and moments later found myself racing through the store marking my selections on the form, fueled by the exciting possibilities of my burgeoning giftaganza: a microwave, an eleven-piece cookware set, a forty-five-inch rear-projection TV, a Chinese vase.

Although at Bergdorf Goodman no one had ever self-registered before, the head of the bridal registry was kind enough to get me special permission to do so. Permission granted, I was given a yellow pad and told to walk around the store and compile a list of the merchandise that I was interested in. Some thirty delicious minutes later, unable to find practical items that would suit me, I had put together a list composed of home furnishings and antiques that distinguished themselves by being both very expensive and very unappealing. But this would be a good test of friendship, I decided; for only a very *dear, dear* friend would buy me the pair of $950 Staffordshire St. Bernards or a $3000 Victorian coal scuttle.

Now I headed for Bloomingdale's. A kind woman in the bridal registry department there gave me a standard form with little boxes marked with categories like CRYSTALS, LIN-ENS, etc., and told me to check the box on the form marked SELF. When I went off into the store to make my selections, I started to feel pangs of guilt about my indulgence at Bergdorf's and decided to try to work within a price range more realistic to my friends' incomes. A no-nonsense New York saleswoman in her late fifties took my form from me when I was finished walking through the store. She looked it over and became, in a word, *flapped.*

"Let me ask you something," she said to me, noticing that I had not signed up for any crockery. "Do you have *dishes?*"

I explained to her that I did. I asked her if they were a popular item in the Bloomingdale's registries.

"Well, it's . . ." She lost her train of thought. *"One* white plastic mug? You want someone to give you one plastic mug? Don't you ever have anyone over?"

"Sometimes," I said, not wanting to get too deep into the particulars of my private life. "But I already have one mug, so I just need the one other," I added.

She looked at me skeptically but decided to let it go.

"Garfield underpants?" she said. "You want someone to go into the boys department and . . ."

"Yes. I like them," I cut her off, anxious not to have the entire bridal registry department apprised of my taste in undergarments.

"Potato chips?" she asked, referring to my brief foray into the Bloomingdale's deli. "What do they come in?"

"A bag," I explained calmly.

"You think someone is going to buy you a *bag* of potato chips for a dollar twenty-five and then have them sent to you?" This was clearly more than she could handle. "Let me ask you something—and I'm not trying to give you a hard time here. But you've only signed up for six things here. I'm sure you have more than six friends."

I nodded.

"Well, then what is the *seventh* person going to buy?"

This seemed an odd question—first she had bullied me about my selections and now she was suggesting that I hadn't made enough of them. I explained to her that I would be very lucky indeed if six of my friends saw fit to take time off from their busy schedules and come buy me gifts. She agreed with this and, after explaining her bafflement with my selections, she ended our discussion by explaining that it would take about ten days for my selections to show up on the computer.

The following week my friend Michael went to Bergdorf's to buy me a gift. Michael expressed to the saleswoman who showed him the merchandise his surprise that my chosen objects could be quite so costly. When Michael explained that he hoped to spend something in the neighborhood of $20 on a gift, the saleswoman went to the trouble of explaining to Michael that *many* people who come to Bergdorf's can't afford the merchandise.

"I don't understand why he picked these things," a slightly confused Michael told the woman. "He . . ."

Laying her hand on Michael's arm in a sympathetic gesture, the saleswoman explained to her young customer, *"He obviously likes antiques."*

Two days later my friend Erica presented me with the bag of potato chips from Bloomingdale's. I was touched by her thoughtfulness and refrained from commenting on the absence of dip.

Michael's efforts, Erica's results—I have been paid a tribute that heretofore I would never have thought imaginable. I am witness to the breadth of my friends' affection for me and, through them, to the breadth of two New York department stores' affection for me. Although I am in other ways a pawn of the marriageocracy, I am less at odds with the likelihood that I will continue to lead a life in which non-birthday and non-Christmas gifts remain unsanctioned.

I have my friends. I have my chips.

WHAT IF UNEMPLOYED ACTORS WORKED IN BANKS INSTEAD OF RESTAURANTS?

10:14 A.M.   Branch manager fires singer-dancer-teller because she wasn't making interesting "choices."

10:49 A.M.   Ingenue teller decorates brass nameplate area with loathsome Pierrot dolls.

11:07 A.M.   Teller gives customer ten singles, vocalizing, "Ten! Tin! Tan! Tawn! Toe! Too!"

1:28 P.M.   Competition among tellers to work at window closest to surveillance camera results in tears and vicious gossip.

1:40 P.M.   Security guard dons bulletproof vest in attempt to protect his "instrument."

2:31 P.M.   Loan officer presses face in sand of canister-type ashtray in preliminary phase of "mask work."

2:39 P.M.   Middle-aged comptroller sees his own wrinkly face reflected in bulletproof glass and wails, "I shall *never* play the Dane!"

2:45 P.M.   Man in torn T-shirt enters bank; surly "Method teller" has arrived for work.

2:59 P.M.   Bank robber's forceful "Put your hands up!" unleashes frenzy of precision dancing.

WHAT IF YOUR DOG DECIDED TO DO A LITTLE REMODELING?

First Week Dog is confused by decorator's suggestion that they cover all walls in bark.

Second Week Dog lodges snout between contractor's legs for genital update.

Third Week Dog becomes irritable and vexed at mention of plaster's "scratch coat."

Fourth Week Dog has all kitchen cabinet doors soldered shut in attempt to thwart chuckwagon.

Fifth Week Dog announces he will paint whole apartment Bone.

WHAT IF THE MAFIA HAD ITS OWN EPONYMOUS FRAGRANCE?

First Week Mobsters copyright slogan "Mafia: For all the men you are . . . and all the men you off."

Second Week *New York Post* runs front-page story with headline GOODSMELLAS!

Third Week Bloomingdale's lines up nine perfume sprayers in a row for gangland-style sprayfest.

Fourth Week Sedan barreling down Brooklyn-Queens Expressway suddenly changes direction: Carmine "the Snake" Persico has forgotten his atomizer.

Fifth Week Overapplication of Mafia short-circuits undercover cop's wire; bathroom stall in Italian restaurant becomes his grisly death crib.

Sixth Week Mob taps actress Talia Shire to be spokesperson for companion scent, Red Sauce.

Seventh Week Informant found bludgeoned to death in trunk of car, Mafia applicator wand placed in mouth.

Eighth Week Large cloud appears over Phoenix skyline: wiseguy in witness relocation program has daubed Mafia on all pulse points.

A Cluttered Existence

Optimist that I am, I have long allowed myself to believe that my life would be ameliorated by having a clutter consultant visit my home. Periodicals, mail, strange and unnecessary requests for money: my apartment is a glowing tribute to my inability to divest.

My feelings about my home are exacerbated by the fact that, having misspent a portion of my adulthood browsing through magazines and coffee-table books that extoll the virtues of the well-appointed residence, I have been bombarded with images of others' propensity and rationales for embracing a starkly minimalist or all-white aesthetic. "[W]e are fascinated by the void," one London couple said of themselves when *House & Garden* photographed their completely barren apartment. "The traditional, unhygienic houses one finds in the U.K., with fabrics and vases and cats everywhere, fill us with horror." A couple in *World of*

Interiors confessed that they had hidden all of their books behind a drilled concrete wall lest the books become a "visual threat" to other objects in the apartment. A home-owner in *House Beautiful* explained her adoption of an all-white aesthetic by saying, "I didn't want to walk in and have a sofa scream at me."

Indeed, the pages of shelter magazines are rife with people who have decided to reduce, to purge, to render their immediate surroundings *simple, simple, simple;* with people who have removed every single item from their apartment except for one slightly rusted eighteenth-century farming implement. "I've actually done it—my own house!" gushed one *World of Interiors* subject who had removed the knobs and handles from all of the drawers in her home; "To me," explained clothing designer Michael Kors to *House & Garden* about the absence of color in his New York apartment, "Cream is a color and Camel is a bright."

Noteworthy about this domestic bulimia (or, as philosopher Jean Baudrillard has called it, "conspicuous austerity") is that it is entirely dependent upon context: to live in a barren apartment in an expensive neighborhood is to suggest that you have a highly refined aesthetic and a lot of friends with names like Tatiana and Winky; to live in a barren apartment in the Bronx is to suggest that you live in a barren apartment in the Bronx.

Unrealistic as it may sound, I suppose that I have always wanted magazines' accounts of others' fervor for minimalism to remove me from my own isolation. When I read Joan Crawford telling *Architectural Digest,* ". . . the first thing

I look for [in an apartment] is what can be ripped out," I want my own enthusiasms to be emboldened by the image of Miss Crawford, in shoulder pads, razing a Manhattan townhouse. When I learn from *House & Garden* that designer Joseph Lembo sleeps in pure white linens because "colored sheets give him headaches," I want to nod knowingly, empathetically. And when *House Beautiful* tells me that, "after hectic days comparing forty shades of crimson and flipping through dozens of sketches in search of the perfect paisley pattern, Linda Allard, the chief designer for Ellen Tracy, does not want to come home to more color and pattern," I want to share my *own* pain—that of coming home after a long workday only to find that Color and Pattern have spent another day in their undershirts, talking to the TV and eating Beer Nuts.

But such is not the case.

Thus my interest in hiring a clutter consultant.

Perhaps, I thought, there is another way. A gentler way.

=

However, before I could unleash said consultant on my home, policy dictated that I attend her class, Letting Go of Clutter. Held by the Learning Annex, a national chain of adult-education schools, the class is the chain's most popular course, with more than 200,000 clutter matriculants. Indeed, paramount among the tens of other books, classes, and services devoted to domestic expurgation, Letting Go is the very jewel of the clutter tiara.

My class was attended by fourteen women and five men,

mostly in their thirties, and was taught by a "career/stress counselor in private practice." A twinkly-eyed, middle-aged woman with ready amounts of alertness and delight, she has the perpetual look of someone who has just been given a large gift. Chief among her tenets of clutter control: Clutter is "whatever *you* think is clutter"; you should work on your clutter fifteen minutes a day, always with a specific goal; you should have folders, each with a label, with which to file loose papers (the teacher, oddly, explained that she has a file labeled "Diseases"). This whole process should be aided by *reframing*—constantly asking yourself, "Do I need it?" "Do I want it?" and "Do I love it?"

Before the class broke for intermission, the teacher encouraged us to find a "support person," someone we would call weekly to discuss clutter goals with. Neatly dodging a woman whose seven interruptions of the teacher in the first hour and a half had suggested a relationship to stackable drawers and the Hold Everything catalog far more empassioned than I thought I could feign interest in on a weekly basis, I approached a friendly-looking, slightly disheveled man who appeared to be in his early sixties. Pointing at the most attractive woman in the room, he explained that he was going to ask her out for coffee and "clutter support." However, he said that if the woman in question turned him down, he would come back to me.

Several minutes later he returned.

"No luck, huh?" I asked.

"Well . . ." he said, looking at the floor.

We exchanged phone numbers.

When the class reconvened, the teacher explained that she was going to lead us on a three-minute visualization, as had been mentioned in the course catalogue. She turned off the overhead lights. Various members of the class reached out to pull their satchels and grocery bags in close to them, the room giving birth to what sounded like several thousand candy wrappers being anxiously crinkled. The teacher encouraged us to breathe deeply. "Relax your feet . . . relax your shins . . . relax your knees," she intoned, slowly working her way up the body until we had achieved an approximation of bodily Jell-O.

Then came the visualization: we were to conjure up first a clutter "problem area" in our homes, then a successful decluttering of that problem area, and finally, the arrival of a photographer from *House Beautiful.* I encountered no difficulty bringing to mind my problem area (that part of my living room floor that my employment as a journalist has led me to saddle with large stacks of periodicals and newspapers); indeed, I even saw myself clearing the area. When the *House Beautiful* photographer arrived, we chatted and had coffee.

It all seemed quite effortless.

But a week later, my clutter remained unchanged.

=

What can be said about my ensuing relationship with my support person can also be said about Chekhov: it started slow, and then it tapered off.

In our first weekly phone call, I learned that he had been

unsuccessfully "sharing goals" over the phone with another support person for five years. When, the next week, neither of us had achieved our goals, he suggested that, if we had still not achieved them by the following week's phone appointment, that we "bookend"—tackle our problem areas immediately upon hanging up—and then call each other (or leave a message on each other's answering machine) to report that we had completed our tasks.

Suddenly the idea that another adult was going to leave a message on my machine explaining that he had moved a pile of magazines off his coffee table was profoundly irritating to me. I thought about our relationship: Did I want it? Did I need it? Did I love it?

Two weeks later, due to mutual apathy, we stopped calling each other.

=

I then spent thirty dollars to join five women at the teacher's apartment (quite tidy) for a monthly two-hour meeting of a support group. "How's this month been?" the teacher asked the three regulars who sat together on the couch.

"A nightmare," said one of them unironically. "A *nightmare* . . ."

Toward the end of the session, the teacher stood and turned off all the lights in the apartment. However, this time around, I was unable to visualize. Plunged into darkness with six female strangers in an unfamiliar apartment, all I could think of was those parties I attended as an adolescent, whereat the installation of a blacklight bulb into a lamp would suddenly render a fellow eight-grader's living room a murky, shadowy "make-out room."

This was not relaxing.

I was having problems letting go.

=

Two weeks later, realizing that I had affected no change to my apartment, I called the teacher and made an appointment for her to perform a one-hundred-dollar, two-hour consultation in my home. When she arrived, I pointed out my problem area: the fifty-five inch stack of old *New York Times*es; the twenty-three inches of *The New Yorker* and *Vanity Fair*; the twenty-two inches of *Esquire, The New Republic,* and *GQ;* the twenty inches of *Harper's* and *Spy;* the seventeen inches of *Entertainment Weekly, House & Garden, Mirabella, Vogue, Metropolitan Home,* and a paranoiac journal called *American Survival;* the twelve inches of *Newsweek;* the twelve inches of *Premiere;* the seven inches of *The New York Observer;* and the four inches of *Variety* and *The Village Voice Literary Supplement.*

"I'm having problems letting go," I explained.

"I can see!" she responded.

She wondered if the publications were related to my work; prevaricating, I told her no, that I tutored English and had no professional need for them.

"I was thinking that I could file to become a branch of the New York Public Library system," I told her.

She smiled indulgently.

I also tried to impress upon her my emotional attachment to the periodicals.

"It's not just a subscription," I explained, "it's a *relationship.*"

She nodded her head sympathetically.

"In fact, some of my best relationships seem to be my subscriptions to magazines," I mumbled.

After I had thrown away all the issues of one magazine that I decided I did not want/need/love (*Newsweek*), dismantled several "nests" of papers and assorted flotsam, and pledged to recycle all of the *New York Times*es, the teacher encouraged me to focus on my "one shots"—magazines that I buy individually at the newsstand.

"Like take *Mirabella,*" she said, picking up an issue of that magazine. "Is this the kind of magazine that you're going to keep and read every article, or just *some* articles?"

I explained that I had bought that issue of the magazine because it contained a profile of a favorite novelist who is not often written about.

"Are you going to keep the article or are you going to let it go?" she asked.

"I could let it go," I said. "I feel like I've done the article."

"So you're ready to let go of the magazine?" she asked.

"I . . . I think I could do that."

"Very interesting. Your words said that, but your nonverbal was a little hesitant."

Some two minutes later, we decided that I would keep the article but throw out the magazine. When the article had been put in its "home" (a folder), the teacher helped me to put all of my issues of *GQ, House & Garden,* and *Vanity Fair* on an empty shelf of my bookshelf, where she felt their smooth, white bindings would be a handsome addition.

When we had finished, I sighed deeply. It had occurred to me that it would be interesting to see how odd the nature of someone's relationship to clutter could be before it would raise eyebrows. Thus did I proceed to tell the teacher that the reason why I had had such difficulty letting go of the magazines and periodicals was because their stacks formed the playground of a special playmate.

"I've always had a little imaginary friend," I told her.

"I did, too," she responded.

"Really?" I asked incredulously.

"Oh, yes."

"He would . . . he likes to spend time here on the magazines," I said of mine, "and that was why I think it was so hard to let go."

"Because his security area was the magazines," she explained. "And *your* security area is the magazines."

"Exactly," I said. "He liked to come with his family and picnic on the back issues of *Harper's.*"

She smiled attentively.

I asked her if her imaginary friend was tied to her problem with clutter; she said no, and that she had had hers when she was young and without siblings.

"Mine is [named] Dr. Kellner," I said.

"*Doctor* Kellner?" she asked, her interest piqued.

"Yes."

"Okay."

"He's a, he's a nose and throat specialist."

"Oh," she exclaimed, "he's a real doctor!"

"He's a specialist," I reiterated.

"A specialist!"

Her expression was equal parts awe and maternal pride—in the world of imaginary friends, I had decidedly married *up*.

Shortly thereafter, we tackled my closet. Then, just before leaving, the teacher enthusiastically encouraged me to come back to the support group.

When she had gone, I cast my eye over the newly created areas of whiteness and organization in my apartment. I saw nooks and crannies where formerly there had only been effluvia and cloggage.

I smiled, experiencing a sensation of satisfaction and completion.

I had let go.

But underneath this sense of completion lurked a tinge of disquiet; disquiet and, perhaps, a touch of remorse about Dr. Kellner.

I would not fully understand these feelings until two weeks later, when I rented a video of the true crime classic *In Cold Blood* and was reacquainted with the name of the family so brutally bludgeoned therein: Clutter.

WHAT IF THE BRONTË SISTERS HAD BEEN
A HEAVY-METAL BAND?

1826 Emily rejects ritual indoctrination in the domestic arts; vows to create a "towering wall of sound."

1835 Charlotte regales parsonage with blistering viola solo.

1837 After signing with P. T. Barnum, Brontë Sisters go on tour opening for the Swedish Nightingale, Jenny Lind.

1842 Anne throws sweat-drenched bonnet into seething concert crowd at Albert Hall.

1847 Emily publishes *Wuthering Heights,* Charlotte publishes *Jane Eyre;* Anne goes into jealous tailspin and starts to experiment with sherry.

1848 Brontë Sisters lock manager, Mrs. Rochester, in attic.

1849 Charlotte returns to public house to trash furniture and have sex with publican.

WHAT IF A PREDOMINANTLY GAY NEIGHBORHOOD WERE SUDDENLY OVERRUN WITH CATTLE?

Drug Store	Holstein buys box of Kleenex in preparation for Tonys broadcast.
Book Store	Brahma Bull scours magazine rack for new porn rag, *Prod*.
Restaurant	Hereford splashes raspberry vinaigrette over painstakingly arranged plate of clover.
Gym	Bull's highly Nautilized brisket elicits epithet "Washboard!"
Theater	Rumor started that prostitute Elsie in song "Cabaret" is actually Borden corporate mascot.
Newsstand	Butcher's diagram of a Black Angus appears as centerfold in *Rawhide*.
Tanning Salon	Guernsey hopes his spots will merge into a tan.

WHAT IF FRANK SINATRA TAUGHT
ENGLISH AT YALE?

September Sinatra assigns lyrics of "Danke Schoen" in attempt to broaden canon.

October Sinatra introduces guest lecturer Harold Bloom as "a big leaguer, the best."

November Sinatra invites coed to downtown New Haven watering hole for intertextuality and highballs.

December Sinatra is late for lecture when pinky ring shreds delicate pages of Norton anthology.

January Sinatra refers to Macbeth as "that bad man Mackie."

February Sinatra exhorts blocked creative-writing major, "Swing, girl!"

March Sinatra delivers paper, "Ode to Joeys: Images of the Baroque in Heatherton and Bishop."

April Conference in New York: Sinatra discusses multiculturalism and gender studies with bodyguard at Copa.

May Sinatra has Yalies deconstruct liner notes to "L.A. Is My Lady."

In Search of . . . *Nubbins*

Obsession begets enterprise. In the early part of 1988, I witnessed a disquieting phenomenon taking place in the pages of *The New York Times:* the otherwise admirable and level-headed restaurant reviewer Bryan Miller was, in his descriptions of various foods, making repeated use of the word *nubbin.* In one review, Mr. Miller explained that radiatore are "little nubbins of pasta with holes in the middle." At Metro restaurant, he encountered "lobster bisque holding sweet nubbins of meat." At Lutèce, he groused, "The nubbins of escargot are lost in their garlicky log of brioche."

Not numbering Mr. Miller amongst my acquaintances, I could only speculate as to what dark, sinister forces were wreaking havoc with his brain each time that he injected his prose with this term; I imagined that, after years of writing about food, he had begun to find *bit, morsel, touch, dollop, soupçon, sprinkle, smidgen, pinch, tidbit, sliver, hint, hair, sprig, dash, shred, whit, driblet, scintilla, trace, tittle, iota, fleck, gobbet, snippet, smithereen, shivereen, shive, snick, chip, nip, snip, flinder, flitter,* and *flake*—like so much of the food forced on him—thoroughly tired and overdone.

But, casting aside my preferred mode of inquiry (idle speculation), I endeavored to give my many nubbin-related questions the full brunt of my journalistic powers. I wondered: Is the term being used by other members of the food community? Is it here to stay? And does it have anything to do with television's beloved fabric-softening bear, Snuggles?

I called twenty-five New York City food experts and identified myself as a journalist hot on the nubbins trail. Neither Barry Wine, the owner-chef of the Quilted Giraffe, nor Milton Parker, the owner of the Carnegie Deli, had ever heard of nubbins. Mr. Parker was quite vehement—"Not even in Jewish. If you want to say 'a pinch,' say 'a pinch'! . . . I'm in this business fifty years, I would *never* use this expression."

Other responses evidenced the term's multiplicity of connotations. Mitchell R. Woo, the chef at the Empire Diner, said, "It sounds like a tiny nodule"; 21 Club chef Anne Rosenzweig responded, "It sounds like little ends of pinkies"; cookbook author Michael McLaughlin thought "Nubbins was a character in a Tolkien book"; Stuart Lichtenstein, the owner of Sardi's, told me, "It sounds like some sort of growth." Mimi Sheraton, Mr. Miller's predecessor at the *Times,* responded, "Nubbins has all the makings of a fast-food chain. You could serve only small, stunted, and ugly food—misshapen mushrooms, mutant potatoes, scraps from other restaurants that you dip in batter and deep-fry. You could hire a staff that looks like nubbins, too."

For Ansell Hawkins, the general manager of the Odeon, and caterer Robert Cacciola, the word had sexual connotations. Mr. Hawkins: "It sounds like duck testicles. Or what a dirty man would call his six-year-old niece: 'Come here, Nubbins!' " Mr. Cacciola: "It sounds like a small penis. It's a Mrs. Field's word. It sounds like a little snacky thing."

=

Shortly after I thought I had finished with my battery of phone calls, I remembered reading about a psychic named Christina Lynn Whited who claimed to be channeling the spirit of the late genius chef James Beard. If anyone would know the score on nubbins, I thought, it would be Mr. Beard—he wrote his first cookbook because he was so frustrated by hostesses serving nothing but what he called "doots" (hors d'oeuvres); his *New Fish Cookery* includes the immortal line, "Here are grunions at their best."

Sadly, however, when I contacted Miss Whited, she said that she would be unable to summon Mr. Beard for me— "James is off working on another cookbook and is generally not available for these kinds of interviews." But she did offer this: "I would imagine that he is familiar with nubbins. . . . Nubbins is very evocative of the fairy domain and the elfin kingdom. It might be appropriate for a childrens' and fairies' cookbook that James and I are writing for eight-year-olds." She concluded, "James's spirit is a rearrangement of other elements from the past. There is a part of us all that is eternal, that is almost always available to be channeled. Nubbins might have a more limited life span."

=

Although the majority of the responses that I received dwelled upon negative connotations, it was clear that I had touched a nerve. After publishing a magazine article in which I detailed Miss Whited's and others' responses, people—readers, friends, and family—began sending me their sightings of the word, forming a sort of unofficial *nubbin* vigil. Eric C. Trefelner, M.D., of Yale University's School of Medicine cited a reference in *Genitourinary Tract Diseases Syllabus* (1986) to a "lower pole nubbin"; a man in Seattle found a cartoon in a 1958 publication called *Six HO Railroads You Can Build* in which an exasperated model-railroad enthusiast (he is holding two ends of track that don't quite reach) cries out, "Oh, Nubbins!"

Nubbins elicited comment and response. Sightings continued to pour in; I learned that my nubbins article had been tacked up over the water cooler in the offices of *Gourmet*. When a colleague's unprompted use of the word in an article in *Rolling Stone* was followed a week later by a TV writer friend's unprompted use of the word on *Sisters*, I started to have a strange, unsettling fear. Namely, that nubbins was an alien being and I was its human host.

To my own mind, nubbins had always conjured up the

image of a calorie-rich snack food. Having misspent a portion of my adolescence in the 1970s as a witless pawn of advertising and food trend, I was all too familiar with a particular type of food product with which food manufacturers flooded the market: a tan, spreadable chemical creme that went by the name Koogle; a boxed cake mix that, when enlivened by water and vinegar, allowed you to make a cake right in the mix's very packaging; a Bundt cake mix whose squeeze packets of blackish paste yielded the disturbing promise of a Tunnel of Fudge.

And so I latched onto the idea of turning my *idée fixe* into a marketable, snacklike confection.

I would launch my own cottage industry.

I would be purged.

=

In its initial stage, a creative project is best approached purely instinctively; thus can the homely offspring of impulse and whim be borne and then promptly abandoned. This dictum at my fore, I jotted down my first approach:

Nubbins

20 Tootsie Rolls, bit in half
½ c. cornmeal
1 egg
A lot of lard

Put egg and ¼ c. water in a bowl; whisk for 1 min. Melt lard in skillet. Soak Tootsie bits in egg mixture,

3–5 min. Roll each in cornmeal. Fry nubbins 2 min. or until cornmeal sac turns golden brown.

The best nubbin is one that is uniformly covered with a thin layer of crispy cornmeal. However, given Tootsie Rolls' inclination, when introduced to heat, to become overly relaxed, this is not always possible. Do not become alarmed when molten Tootsie bursts from its sac; simply scoop the bubbling mass up and, putting it on a plate, manipulate it into a pleasing shape. When reconstructing nubbins on the plate, the ratio between Toosie Roll and cornmeal is entirely at your own discretion; however, avoid serving anyone a big clot of burnt sac.

After diligently carrying out these instructions one afternoon in my kitchen, I discarded this recipe; its results were not delicious.

Over the next eight months I tried some nineteen different nubbin variants. Almost all were sweet; all were bite-sized. I traversed the world of yummy, snacky eatables, from corn puffs to pecan bars to marshmallow-filled profiteroles. An episode of *Nova* helped me with terminology: I learned that the texture of a snack food when it is in your mouth is referred to as its *mouth-feel;* the gradations of resistance it offers while being eaten (as measured by the electrical activity in the mouth's muscles) is referred to as its *chew profile.*

My breakthrough occurred shortly after I started making my own French bread. Buttons of French bread, each with a crackly, egg-white-washed crust, were slightly salty and utterly delicious. The slight crunchiness of the crust gave way to a resilient, airy cushion that held up, glutenous bite after glutenous bite: a chew profile from Heaven. Then, putting a pastille of milk chocolate in the middle of each hank of dough before cooking, I gave birth to my brain-child.

Bread and chocolate: a classic. Success.

=

There remained, of course, the question of whether or not my fledgling would succeed in the marketplace. It is one thing to be enamored of your own creative output, one thing to find yourself, as I had, standing at your kitchen sink in your underpants at three o'clock one morning rhapsodically snarfeling down your latest breakthrough, and it is another to convince a total stranger that he and his corporation should part with their millions.

For the same reason that producers of TV series generally do not accept scripts that people send to them unsolicited in the mail, most corporations won't consider or develop unsolicited ideas for new products—they run the risk of a lawsuit if they are already developing a similar idea in-house and then bring it out on the market after receiving an unsolicited proposal for a similar product.

And yet . . . there are always exceptions.

I wrote proposal letters to sixteen of the country's more visible snack manufacturers, begging them "to make an exception in this instance." Among the companies were

Kraft, Hunt-Wesson, Nabisco, Hershey, Keebler, Brach's, Grand Metropolitan (Pillsbury, Häagen-Dazs), Continental Baking (Wonder, Hostess), and Mars (Official Snack Food Sponsor of the 1992 Olympic Games).

> *I have developed a highly delicious and unusual new snack food which would be the perfect accompaniment to your line of products. I call these tiny mouthfuls Nubbins.*
>
> *I also have an idea for an exciting Nubbins promotional display in stores: I envision a 9' tall volcano which would gently ooze Nubbins' rich, fulsome filling. Each interruption of the lava's flow would release a large, suspended net which would drop over unsuspecting shoppers in other parts of the store, suddenly trapping them in an eerie snack limbo. Once the shopper had been "netted," he would be approached by the volcano's attendant, who, dressed as a shadowy figure called Count Snackula, would bear a tray of steaming hot Nubbins.*
>
> *To play the role of the Count, I suggest either the little boy from* Home Alone *or my allergist, Dr. Napel.*

When Brach's wrote back, they did not request Dr. Napel's phone number. However, they did send me a "confidential disclosure waiver." This form letter, written by Brach's attorney, suggested that, after I had engaged the services of either an attorney or a notary public, I resubmit my idea. I also received a similar letter from Eagle Snacks.

Although I realized that these letters were probably sent to anyone who submitted letters (when I later wrote the two companies using another name and said that I had invented a cookie called Lacey Unmentionables, Eagle expressed interest, but Brach's did not), these two missives were as sightings of land amidst an ocean of rejection. I excitedly sent off a proposal for a mass-market version of Nubbins: a canister, similar to the ones containing Pillsbury Poppin' Fresh products, would be filled with pieces of dough wrapped around disks of chocolate, which consumers would cook on a griddle.

When I had heard nothing after ten days, I upped the ante by sending Brach's and Eagle an idea for a TV ad:

Possible TV Ad for "Nubbins"

In the foreground we see a group of thirty or so hungry, waifish children dressed in rags. Dickensian squalor. In the background, Nubbins are being made by a man wearing a hat emblazoned with the Nubbins logo. The children, addressing the man, sing an impassioned version of Neil Young's rock 'n' roll classic, "Southern Man."

> Nubbins Man, better keep your head,
> Don't forget what your cookbook says.
> Nubbin change gonna come at last,
> Just keep those bread sacs from burnin' fast.

(Children undulate during guitar solo, striking poses of intense need and desire. A solo vocalist breaks loose from the rabble and sings directly to camera.)

I've had cotton candy, I've had Jax,
Appalling "Lite" ranch chips and other snacks,

*(Then, suddenly drawing a bloodied knife from beneath
his rags)*

Swear by God I'll stab them in the back!

*(Then, as the electric guitars start to pulsate and build
in fiery climax, the children all rush up to the stove with
looks of abject craving.)*

I hear fryin'
And eggshells crackin'.
How long? How long?
Ah! Nubbins Man!

Seven weeks later I received a form rejection letter from
Brach's corporate counsel; a week after that I received a
letter from Eagle stating that my idea was being held "for
future consideration." After waiting another month and a
half, I called Eagle and spoke with a young woman in the
marketing dept. In an attempt to stoke the fire, I told the
woman, "I've had some interest about Nubbins from a
movie studio. I'm not at liberty to say *which* studio—but
it's Disney."

She explained that it was almost certain that the company
would not be pursuing my idea.

"I think they're thinking along the California Raisin–
Gummi Bears lines," I said, referring, in the first instance,
to the wrinkly entity that went from being a food to a
commercial to a TV show to a toy and, in the latter in-

stance, to the chewy delight that went from being a candy to a TV show about and sponsored by the candy.

"We have to be really neutral and this is kind of explicit in parts," she said. "We go through an ad agency. . . ."

"They didn't like the song I submitted—they thought that was a little frightening," I said. "But I think the opportunities for ancillaries are very exciting—the T-shirt, the gimme cap, the fragrance."

She explained that my idea would be kept on file, adding, "but I don't want to get your hopes up."

"So you weren't really interested," I said, forlorn that she couldn't grasp the overwhelming beauty of a fragrance vial bearing the name Nubbins.

"The interest is always there in anything. But as to the *degree* of interest . . ."

=

When the reticence with which my brainchild was met by the corporate world began to gnaw at my confidence and enthusiasm, I decided to approach the marketplace in a more direct manner. It had long occurred to me that the Nubbins might translate well to the idiom of the street fair. Shaved ice drenched with syrups whose flavors are advertised as "cherry, lemon, or blue"; pieces of fried dough glistening with tragic dermatological consequence—this might be the very backdrop against which to showcase my Nubbins to their best advantage.

I set my sights on the Feast of San Gennaro, the street fair that draws over 3 million New Yorkers and visitors to

Little Italy each September. Knowing that I had neither the stamina nor the courage (nor, for that matter, the vendor's license) to have my own booth for the entire eleven-day run of the Feast, I decided instead that I would try to join forces with another vendor. I called the San Gennaro Society; a man with a hoarse, New Yorky rasp told me that all prospective vendors should report to the "trailer office" at 195 Hester Street between ten A.M. and five P.M. on September third, a few days before the Feast was to commence. Hying myself to this location on the appointed day, I climbed three wooden steps and knocked on the door of the trailer parked on the side of the street. A teenage boy opened the door for me, revealing a plump woman in her sixties adorned with a royal blue sweatshirt and with two pink hair curlers atop her head.

"Can I help you?" she asked, her voice a mixture of warmth and gravel.

"Yes. Is this the place where people who want to be vendors come?"

"What do you sell?"

"I've, unh . . . I've invented a new snack food."

"Oh, really?" she asked, not all that interested. "What is it?"

"They're called Nubbins. It's like French bread with melted chocolate inside it. I'm wondering if it'd be possible to supply it to someone who would sell it at his stand."

She looked concerned.

"It's French bread with chocolate?" she asked.

I nodded.

She visibly shuddered.

"Oooh," she said, grimacing, "you just sent *shivers* down my spine."

"Well, you've had croissants with chocolate inside them before, right?" I tried to reason. "It's like that." I described their appearance as "lovely."

She looked down at the floor as if averting the sight of blood. "That would be very difficult to get someone to resell."

Several seconds later, there was a knock on the trailer's door. The boy opened the door and, seeing a young Asian man, yelled, "Buffalo wings!"

The Asian man chuckled and said, "Right." The woman guided him to a table where a man in his sixties, previously unseen by me, was stationed. This older man greeted the younger man, "Hello, Buffalo Wings," and then asked him to fill out a form.

The woman returned to me and said, "Now are we through?"

I said that I supposed we were and left.

Mulberry Street was dotted with vendors' booths in varying states of readiness for the Feast. Having decided that—if given the chance—I would cook my Nubbins on a cast-iron griddle that I would put on top of a vendor's grill, I proceeded to ask three different vendors if they would let me set up shop with them. I offered them what I thought was an exorbitant amount of money—three hundred dollars a day. They all declined. Their responses: "It wouldn't work out," "I can't give up the grill space," and "I've already got the sausage."

=

Before I returned to the site of the Feast to plead my case again the next week, I changed the recipe for Nubbins. Not sure that I would be able to sell them at the Feast, I had begun to pursue getting my own vendor's license from the Board of Health's permit division. However, since the application for such prohibited the sale of "home-prepared foods," I became anxious that my home-prepared French bread might lead to my arrest. At the time, a friend of mine had taken to making the Italian bread focaccia by buying pizza dough at a pizza parlor (most will do this, charging three or four dollars for enough dough to make one pie), then taking it home and covering it with olive oil, parmesan, and herbs. Thus, engaging in the kind of last-minute retooling that can so often elevate the merely mediocre into the truly brilliant, I was now buying pizza dough at pizza parlors, wrapping hanks of it around disks of Droste bittersweet chocolate, and then cooking the resultant bundle in a little oil on a griddle.

=

When I returned to the Feast, it was with some of the feelings of anxiety and protectiveness evidenced in mothers who are interviewing prospective nannies. Having, for the past nine months, nurtured my creation within the confines of my own home, I had now reached the potentially heart-breaking stage whereat I must expose my progeny to the harsh light of the outside world. Walking down the length of Mulberry Street, I saw huge mounds of peppers and onions and coiled sausage cooking on grills; I saw photo booths equipped with zany, oversized props; I saw many, many Portosans.

But I did not see a home for Nubbins.

And then, suddenly, amidst the smoke and the jeering and thronging masses, my eyes fixated: it was Buffalo Wings. Standing at a booth emblazoned Big City Wings, he was using a squeeze bottle to lather chicken legs and breasts with an herby, oily goo. I walked over and awkwardly introduced myself to him; he was warm and friendly but did not recognize me from the trailer. I made my proposal; he was not uninterested.

"Did you get approval from the Board of Health?" he asked.

"No," I said. Then, anxious to appear legitimate, I added, "But I'm a caterer."

He suggested I return the following day with a sample, saying, "I'll try it and if we like it, I'll sell it." He cautioned, "Just bring a little. Don't bring too much."

I awoke the following day with the issues of display and presentation throbbing in my mind. I put six warm Nubbins on a plate, wrapped the samples and the plate in Saran Wrap, and put them in an unused cardboard bakery box. While making my way over to Little Italy in a cab, I nervously lifted the Saran Wrap off of the plate and flapped it up and down so as to reduce potentially merchandise-obscuring condensation.

When I got to Buffalo Wing's stand, he was busy with customers; he told me to leave the samples and that he would call me with his decision the following day. I suddenly realized that I had not yet described to him the makeup of a Nubbin. Operating under the assumption that the average person wants to be forewarned that, when he bites into Food Item Number One, he will discover the hidden presence of Food Item Number Two, I bit one of the samples in half and said, "See, there's chocolate inside." The part of my brain that is a storage area for unctuous pronouncements prompted me to add, "Mmm . . . chocolatey and good."

=

Buffalo Wings did not call me the next day. Nor the day after that. In short, Buffalo Wings did not call me at all. Frustrated and forlorn, I contemplated abandoning the project altogether. I contemplated going and having a scene with him. I contemplated filling a shopping bag with pizza dough and then abandoning it on the #4 train to the Bronx.

But instead I went back to the Feast. At a booth with many colorful signs advertising Steak Giambotta, Chicken Savoy, and fruit salad, I explained to the large, Italian-American proprietor that I had invented a new snack food and was eager to give it a trial run. He told me to return in fifteen minutes and talk to his partner. When I returned,

I met the partner, a short, cocky man in his forties whom I will call Sal.

"So you think they'll do good with sausage and chicken?" Sal asked after I had made my proposal.

"Yeah," I said. "They're good. And no one else is making anything like them."

I sweetened the deal by offering Sal and his partner half of my profits. Sal said that they would have to discuss it; he told me to come back in fifteen minutes.

When I returned, Sal acknowledged my arrival but then proceeded to ignore me for some six minutes. When he had finished showing a young male employee how to make Chicken Savoy, Sal told me that he wasn't sure if he would have enough grill space for me. I explained to him the dimensions of my griddle; this seemed to calm him. Becoming increasingly aware that Sal rarely looked me in the eyes, I spent another four or five awkward minutes standing outside the booth while he alternately ignored me and asked me questions. When he finally agreed to my proposal, he said, "So come on Thursday at eleven-thirty, bring me the three, and we'll see how it goes. If it works then we'll run with it." Eager to secure the agreement, I suggested that I bring half of "the three" the following day, Wednesday, as a down payment. He agreed. When I gave him the money the next day, we decided that I would start working on Thursday afternoon. He gave me permission to put a display on the front counter, saying, "You know what you do? You get a paper plate, fold it in half, decorate it nice."

=

When I reported for work on Thursday at the appointed hour, Sal was nowhere in sight. The booth was being manned by a young man in his early twenties named Kenny. Not sure what my rights were in this situation, I timidly entered the already-crowded fifteen-by-ten-foot area of the stand and started to unpack my supplies. After putting four of my five orders of pizza dough in the stand's refrigerator, I quickly started to wrap disks of chocolate with dough. After I had fashioned twenty of them, I hung up my sign, a fifteen-by-fourteen-inch piece of white posterboard, onto which I had put two-and-three-inch-high red vinyl letters reading:

NUBBINS

THE *FRIENDLY* SNACK

Underneath this, in smaller lettering, was MELTED BITTER-SWEET CHOCOLATE INSIDE A HOT BREAD POCKET . . . 2 FOR 50 CENTS.

When Sal arrived, he did not address me directly, opting instead to mumble "Hiya" to both Kenny and me. When Kenny told Sal that the two workers from the last shift had taken the money they made back to "the restaurant" (the workers and the equipment, I would later learn, came from a restaurant in New Jersey), Sal slammed the side of the booth with his hand, causing it to rock.

"Those goddamn motherfuckers!" he yelled. "Fuckin' idiot—he doesn't know *what* he's doing!"

He then kicked a cardboard box that was lying on the floor. It crashed against the side of the wooden stand, emitting a hollow boom. I scurried to the far side of the stand, suddenly occupying myself with a piece of dough.

"Yo, Henry—you got that money?" Sal asked.

Once given the money, Sal left for about twenty minutes. While he was gone, another employee—a dark, lovely woman in her late thirties named Linda—showed up and took an interest in my wares.

"Chocolate in bread?" she asked, her eyes widening with amazement. "That's *obscene.*"

While Sal was gone, I put some Nubbins on the griddle, which was some four inches away from six or seven chicken breasts slowly cooking on the grill. I tried to work as gingerly as possible lest I incur sensitive sac rupture. I also availed myself of the opportunity to put out my display on the counter. I had taken a postcard of a dewy-eyed, sequined, choker-wearing Barbra Streisand, circa *A Star Is Born,* and, in small vinyl lettering, all capitals, written NUB-BINS across her forehead. Then I positioned this postcard into the edges of an aluminum-foil dish so that it stood straight up; I anchored the dish with three cooked Nubbins.

Both Sal and Linda had expressed a desire to taste my wares. Upon serving them each a Nubbin, I quickly returned to my griddle, anxious that my tenancy at the booth might be subject to their approval. Just then I heard Linda gasp as Sal shouted, "Goddamnit!" I winced. Sal continued, "Henry, you're out of here. Pack it up—this thing just *came* all over me!" I turned around to look, whereupon I saw Linda quickly grab a napkin and Sal—fortunately—began to laugh; he had bitten into the Nubbin too vehemently and now the treat's liquid center was spread out all over his shirt front. Moments later, Linda expressed her enthusiasm for the Nubbin's taste and asked for a second.

Between four-thirty and five-thirty, I sold only three Nubbins; however, in my own defense, I must point out that the crowd was fairly sparse.

"They're good," one of my customers enthused. "Sort of French."

At about five, Sal went outside the booth and started to wipe the front counter with a sponge. He looked slightly askance at my Streisand display. I became very conscious of the fact that my display was far more involved than a paper plate folded in half.

"Is this Barbra Streisand?" he asked.

I confirmed that it was.

"What for?" he asked dubiously.

"It'll bring people in," I said. "Curiosity."

Sal recommenced wiping, a pensive, slightly displeased look on his face. Would this, I wondered, be the last straw? Then Sal stopped wiping. He walked over to the display. He picked it up. Then, turning it so that it was facing me, he advised me, "You should have gotten one of her nude."

I nervously agreed with him, not bothering to outline for him the difficulty inherent in obtaining such a thing.

As the crowd began to swell, Kenny, Linda, and I began to yell the names of our various wares in an increasingly loud fashion. When, at one point, Linda included "Nubbins!" in her spiel, Sal whispered something in her ear, and thereafter she did not do it again.

I experienced a steady trickle of customers. About one out of every three people who came to look at the griddle or the display would end up making a purchase. I wondered if I wasn't losing customers because of the Nubbins' appearance; their casings continued to crack, causing the dark, mottled chocolate to be exuded in a manner that was unlovely. I threw many a Nubbin away. And I started to use more dough.

Taking my cue from Kenny and Linda, I also began to take an increasingly aggressive approach to sales. When a woman sidled up to the grill and, speaking to a space equidistant between Kenny and me, said, "I'll have two," I asked, "Two Nubbins?"

"No," she said. "Two chicken sandwiches, please."

"Would you like a nice Nubbin to go with that?" I asked.

"No, thank you."

"They're nice. They're hot and nice."

"No, just chicken, please."

"Maybe after dinner you'll have some."

"Yeah, maybe after dinner."

Later, when a woman in her twenties looked at my sign and said, "Nubbins? Oh God—my boyfriend's in a band called Nubbin," I tried to impress upon her the potential enjoyment to be wrought from Nubbins' use as a "gigging snack." This was not interesting to her.

=

Although Kenny and I were so closely stationed together at the grill that our elbows repeatedly rubbed against one another's, we coexisted peaceably. The lavishing of vinegar and spices onto the chicken parts was effected with a minimum of spray or fallout to my area. However, three times during the evening, Sal—who had taken to referring to my wares as "your, uh, your *muffins*"—briefly stood in for Kenny. With a dramatic flourish that I can only imagine was intended to excite comment and interest from the crowd, Sal would pour vinegar from a height some three feet above the grill. Herb-flecked vinegar would splash onto my griddle; a huge cloud of smoke would pour forth from the chicken. After several of these hot, vinegary blasts had buffeted against my face and person, I was left with the distinct impression that Sal was trying to kipper me.

=

At about eight-thirty the crowd in the street doubled, its swollen size now sometimes causing the stand to rock slightly. In my rush to keep up with consumer demand, I began to make increasingly large Nubbins—originally the size of Ping-Pong balls, they had now ballooned to the size of tennis balls. One man said to me, "That's only twenty-five cents? That's too cheap. I'm not sure it will be any good." (For reasons unclear to me, this comment prompted the woman accompanying him to launch into an extended riff on the word *nuppins*.)

At one point I looked up from my griddle and saw that two women who had been admiring the picture of Miss Streisand were now eating the Nubbins that were sitting in the foil dish.

"Ladies," I said. "That's the display you're eating."

"Oh, these aren't samples?" one of them responded.

"No, you're eating the display."

The woman looked at her and her friend's half-eaten portions with slight horror.

"Are they, are they . . . okay?" she asked.

Curbing my impulse to tell her that she had just eaten a highly polished piece of wood, I assured her that she had eaten only the highest quality baked good. Then, in the name of consumer relations, I refused payment.

I had started to feel slightly guilty that some of the customers were being shortchanged. Sudden, intense waves of customers—immediately followed, of course, by long stretches of total inactivity—sometimes prohibited me from maintaining the level of quality control so essential to the production of comestibles. When a recently served customer broke through the ranks of a family of four that I was serving, showed me his sad, half-eaten Nubbin, and asked, "Is it supposed to be raw dough with a lot of, like, *burnt shit* on the bottom?" it was the harried middle-manager in me who calmly explained to him that yes, indeed, that was the desired effect.

For the most part, however, my customers were very satisfied. I had two repeat customers; one man had four portions wrapped up to take home to his wife. One of the repeat customers, having had two of the smaller Nubbins at the beginning of the evening, returned later to find that Nubbins had trebled in size. After learning that the new, larger Nubbin had the same amount of chocolate in it as the old one did, she admonished me, "You should control how much chocolate is in them."

At about ten-thirty I suddenly realized that I had run out of dough. I thought about rushing off to a pizza parlor and buying more, but somehow, having sold forty-five Nubbins, having had two repeat customers, I felt complete.

"I'm packing up shop," I told Sal.

I started to hand him the eleven dollars that was his percentage of my profit, but he told me to keep it.

=

Bit by bit, I wage my campaign. Admittedly, there is still ground to be covered: You do not see Nubbins served with coffee at the conclusion of 12-Step meetings. You do not hear kindergarten children parroting the Nubbins jingle or tag line. You do not associate the word *nubbins* with members of the law enforcement community.

But one day—one day in the not-too-distant future, if will and determination are rewarded in this lifetime—all this will change. One day you will be strolling down Aisle 3 of your local supermarket when suddenly a large net will drop over you, and a hoary, disheveled allergist will approach bearing a platter of delectable goodies.

Embrace this man. Embrace him and his offerings. For it is only then that you will savor the fruit of obsession.

WHAT IF YOUR MOTHER LIVED AT THE PLAYBOY MANSION?

11:00 A.M. Mom's eyes well with tears when Miss May says her "Likes" include candles, honesty, and sharing.

11:54 A.M. Mom assumes that coke spoon she found under sofa cushion is instrument used in nail care.

12:01 P.M. Mom confuses other Mansion guests with repeated references to Hef's ex, "Barley Bensen."

3:34 P.M. Miss June cuts phone sex short when she realizes Mom is listening in on upstairs extension.

6:40 P.M. Mom leaves Jacuzzi area to get Miss January a sweater.

1:01 A.M. Mansion guests pile onto Hef's bed to screen videos; Mom launches into lengthy reminiscence about when movie admission was a nickel.

WHAT IF A FOUR-YEAR-OLD AMISH BOY GOT LOST IN THE CONDÉ NAST BUILDING?

Glamour   Editor notes trend: Farmers are getting younger!

Brides   Boy drools on furniture in lobby; shrieking receptionist momentarily loses fake English accent.

Self   Receptionist tells boy that she wishes he were a can of Tab.

Vanity Fair   Assistant editor tells boy that most Amish people are not famous.

GQ   Swishy art assistant tells colleague that, yes, boy is only four, but he has the *body* of a six-year-old.

Mademoiselle   Beauty editor smiles at speck of mud on boy's cheek: assumes boy has been playing with samples of new fruit-based masque.

Vogue   Assistant publisher ashes cigarette over boy's head: assumes boy's straw hat is large mobile thatched ashtray.

WHAT IF YOUR LANDLORD WERE
NOMINATED FOR AN OSCAR?

February 15 Elated landlord appears on local news wearing ice pack and grubby bathrobe.

March 3 Landlord buys auto-pen to sign all new leases "Love ya!"

March 29 Landlord forces tears on Barbara Walters special when asked about rent hike.

March 29 Geena Davis tells landlord she is cold; landlord bangs on pipes of Dorothy Chandler Pavilion with wrench to create illusion of impending warmth.

March 29 Landlord tells Special Effects copresenter that he will announce name of winner "gratis."

March 29 Defeated landlord attends Swifty Lazar bash; tells Shelley Winters he loved her in *The Tenant*.

2 Yrs. Later Landlord moves to Canoga Park; takes job at Taco Bell.

Games of Chintz

Although my lack of passion and aptitude for decorating has led me to outfit most of my apartments in a style that might be best described as Early Newstand, I have long been intrigued by the earnestness and zeal with which others address themselves to the pursuit of domestic loveliness. Thus when, in the past, I have visited decorator showhouses—those events at which a dozen or so interior designers each decorate a room in a single residence no one will ever inhabit, the ticket sales to which are given to charity—it is less because I have a long-held fascination with Marie Antoinette recamiers and Louis XIV sconces than because I am loath to pass up any opportunity to overhear the promiscuous use of the phrase *yummy chintz*.

Indeed, promiscuity is the leitmotiv of decorator showhouses. Decorators who work on showhouses use their own money to pay for whatever furniture or supplies they are unable to borrow or have donated; some of them, anxious to reap the maximum benefit in publicity and job referrals, spend as much as $150,000 on a room. Given that the decorator decorates a showhouse room to his own specifications and not a client's, there are fewer constraints on his sense of the fabulous. It becomes too easy for him to ignore the little voices that admonish "Less, darling— *much, much* less": Several years ago, a decorator at a New Jersey showhouse swathed the walls and contents of an entire room in fake fur and called it the Furmality Room; at a 1993 Saratoga Springs, New York, showhouse with the theme "Let Music Fill the Air," recordings of Brahms and Beethoven emanated from a nonworking toilet. And at a recent showhouse in Massachusetts, Jamie Gibbs upholstered the frames of two dozen cafeteria chairs with moss, explaining "as it ages, the moss will turn gold to match the tassels."

Sometimes the excess is of a more esoteric nature. "This is not a complete room," read Thierry Despont's description of one of his two 1991 French Designer Showhouse rooms in honor of the French poet Rimbaud, "but broken pieces, a wall here, a mirror there, and then a dark cabinet that does not connect but is there, as a fragment, Rimbaud's last refuge. A flying tub, a stellar sphere, accounting books and images of slaves. The walls, the obscure cabinet, the galaxy . . . it is as if the wind of poetry had shattered a room." The larger of Despont's rooms featured a winged bathtub; the smaller contained a sink filled with spears and twigs.

Standing in the room that had been shattered by the

wind of poetry, this 1991 French Designer Showhouse visitor was filled with a vague sense of loss; it seemed that none of the decorator's startling expressions of style would translate to my own apartment. But upon further inspection, I realized that I might make use of the larger room's hemplike carpeting (which, a decorator visiting the showhouse told me later, was sisal matting). However, when I asked the lacquered, well-heeled volunteer in charge of the room what it was exactly that covered the floor, she told me, "I think it's a doormat."

"Really?" I asked with genuine surprise.

"Yes," she added. "I think it's a big doormat."

I suppose that if my curiosity about the matting had been profound, I might have consulted the glossy brochure that had been handed to me at the entrance to the showhouse. However, I try never to read these publications, as they tend to disappoint, creating the false impression that you are about to experience something very, very funny—juxtapositions of style are referred to as *ironic;* arrangements, *witty;* individual pieces, *tongue in cheek.* Try as I might, I never seem able to grasp the full comic potential of what is being described. But then again, perhaps you cannot force these things. With the good furniture, the really *funny* furniture, a boffo comedy experience probably just sneaks up on you—one minute you're looking at an ormolu-mounted rosewood sideboard, the next your lunch from Le Cirque is coming right out your nose.

=

When showhouse rooms are dedicated to famous people who, unlike Rimbaud, are still living, the essential voyeuristic conceit of showhouses (walking around someone else's house when he is not home) is heightened by the subject's standing in society (walking around some *famous* person's house when he is not home). This was the case at a showhouse in Rye, New York, where Jean P. Simmer's room, At Ease—its ceiling covered with camouflage from a tank that had been in the Gulf—paid homage to Norman Schwarzkopf. However, in this instance the thrill of the illicit was tinged with terror; for while the room was dappled with Schwarzkopf's favorite beverages (Johnnie Walker Red, Diet Pepsi), it was also equipped with what appeared to be his favorite playthings (glazed hand grenades).

Entertaining People, a ten-year-old Washington, D.C., showhouse that raises funds for the Washington Home, a health-care facility for the terminally ill, puts its own spin on this strange form of celebrity worship by actually pairing decorators up with celebrities or government VIPs meant to be the subjects of their rooms. These rooms tend to focus on one of three fascinating themes: how the VIP entertains, how the VIP *wishes* he could entertain, or how the *decorator* wishes the VIP could entertain. The VIP lends personal possessions from his home: When former drug czar William Bennett and his wife worked with a local decorator to create a treehouse inside Washington's Mayflower Hotel, where the showhouse is held, Bennett lent his guitar and volunteered to make an audiocassette of himself singing and playing guitar with one of his sons. Meant as a place where the Bennetts could picnic with their children, the treehouse was stocked with cookies, hot dogs, and jars filled with bugs. And for a room extolling the virtues of the equestrian life, Senator John Warner provided his own custom-made English riding boots, his riding hat and habit, suede jacket, riding silks, and a pair of velvet slippers; the decorator upholstered the walls in wool the color of jodhpurs.

The decorators are clearly entranced by their subjects. When Entertaining People asked decorator Victor Shargai to decorate a room for Kelly McGillis on the theme of "A Whimsical Dinner at Eight," Shargai created a room based on the old motorsailer that McGillis and her husband Fred hope one day to buy and restore. Shargai explained in the show's catalogue, "The on-board scenario would find Kelly in the galley (sneaking glances out the portholes at the seascapes she loves so much) while Fred and friends join her as she cooks one of her 'al dente' wonders. What a life!" (What a life, indeed—*The Kelly McGillis Story: A Passion for Pasta.*)

But of all of the showhouse rooms fueled by this unsavory form of voyeurism, few match Katherine Stephens's re-creation of the room thought to be Franklin D. Roosevelt's childhood room. Says Stephens, "Being disabled doesn't mean that you have to live in surroundings that are unattractive." According to a photo caption from *Interior Visions: Great American Designers and the Showcase House*—oddly, given that Roosevelt did not contract polio until he was almost forty—the showhouse room was outfitted with an electric bed and a remote control for the TV, curtains, and telephone. The caption added, "Below, the flat, low-pile industrial carpet facilitates movement, avoiding drag with the wheelchair; most important, it is static-free."

As the wheelchair aged, it no doubt turned gold to match the tassels.

NINE-TO-FIVING

"You'll Never Groom Dogs in This Town Again!"

Spitting is prohibited in subway cars mainly to:

  a) encourage politeness
  b) prevent spread of disease
  c) reduce the cost of cleaning cars
  d) prevent slipping

  From the Telephone Maintainer civil service test

Assume that, while a [Bridge and Tunnel] Officer is collecting a toll from a motorist, the Officer sees a child tied up in the rear of the car. Of the following, the best thing for the Officer to do is to:

  a) ignore what has been seen and continue
     collecting tolls
  b) try to delay the car and signal for assistance

   c) reach into the car and untie the child

   d) tell the driver that he cannot use the bridge unless he unties the child

> *From a preparation guide for the Bridge and Tunnel*
> *Officer civil service test*

The proper technique for selling floral designs involves:

   a) ignoring customers when they are waiting for service

   b) being assertive, taking no nonsense from the customer

   c) treating the customer the way you want to be treated

   d) calling the customer "honey" or "dear"

> *From an exam given by the Rittner's School*
> *of Floral Design in Boston, Massachusetts*

In earlier, simpler times, you became established in a trade by following a steady path from apprentice to journeyman to master. You matured into a trusted artisan through a natural process, and you did not need to be worried about becoming "certified" and filling in computer-readable answer bubbles with a number-two pencil and responding "true" or "false" on a psychological test to the statement "I prefer tall women." No, a blacksmith was a blacksmith because he was a blacksmith; chandlers chandled and wheel-wrights wrought wheels. In today's superrationalized, post-industrial world, however, we trust numbers more than experience, so to qualify for almost any money-making endeavor, from lawyer to interior decorator to cement mason, you may be obliged to take a test. There is a Certified Picture Framers examination. There is an Aerobics Instructors test.

In an attempt to identify exactly what employers and professional organizations are looking for in their employees and members—and, incidentally, to identify exactly what work I might be suited for other than the underration-alized and basically preindustrial labor of freelance writ-ing—I took thirty-one official or practice tests. The tests ranged from tests for bartenders, postal machine mechanics, radio announcers, and travel agents to tests for addiction specialists, geologists, foreign service officers, and FBI agents. (I did not take the exam for state troopers, however, having taken offense at some of the questions in a prepara-tion guide for that test: "When driving a full-sized car, are you tall enough to see over the steering wheel?" "When standing next to a full-sized car, can you easily see over the top?" "Can you climb over a full-sized sedan either length-wise or from side to side?" The writers of the test seemed to suspect me of being a dwarf.)

My results were not always encouraging; I passed only three tests.

There is not yet a test for freelance writers, of course. It occurs to me that perhaps this is just as well.

SO YOU WANT TO BE A COSMETOLOGIST

In addition to a written test that includes questions on bacteriology, trichology, dermatology, and histology, aspiring cosmetologists in New York State must pass a three-hour-long practical exam. At the busy, dark premises of the Wilfred Beauty Academy at Broadway and Fifty-fourth Street, I took the first four of seven parts of the mock version of the practical exam that Wilfred students must pass before taking the state board examination.

I entered the classroom area, its air redolent with the aroma of singed hair and perfumey fluorocarbons. I joined a group of about thirty white-lab-coat-wearing students who were under the tutelage of the obdurate Ms. Valentine. A short, middle-aged Hispanic woman with full, round cheeks, Ms. Valentine has a slightly regal bearing and luxuriant blonde hair—the empress dowager of Wella Balsam. But upon introducing herself to me she explained, "They call me the Drill Sergeant."

Pleasantries dispensed with, she reached into the three-foot-tall wooden cabinet in which wigs are dried and pulled out a male rubber mannequin head with slightly chiseled, epicene facial features. Its hair was done up in curlers and covered with a hairnet. Then, with a clamping device, Ms. Valentine used her impressive strength to briskly attach the head to the worktable closest to the wig dryer.

Ms. Valentine barked out the command to begin the first part of the exam—the "comb-out"—and then urged us to be assiduous about "relaxing the set." Upon seeing that other students were "effilating" (teasing) their heads' hair with combs, I followed suit; but upon snagging and almost breaking one of the comb's teeth in the resultant tangle, I decided that this was not the proper avenue to hair relaxation. I recommenced with a brush. When a bell sounded at the conclusion of the twenty-five minutes, I had fashioned a sort of churning mass of blondeness—Gunther Goebbel-Williams after having strayed too close to an air duct. Ms. Valentine strode around the room and, jabbing her finger into some coiffures, briefly combing others, took notes. Her look of unenthused calm suggested a high level of professionalism.

For the hair-shaping phase of the exam, I was given a water sprayer, plastic clips, shears, and a female mannequin head with long, straight brown hair. Handing me an illustration of a head of hair sectioned into four quadrants and one encircling fringe, Ms. Valentine explained that I would have thirty minutes to "section, remove excess bulk, and blend." This sounded like a tall order. Indeed, it was—I spent twenty-four minutes effecting a fringe and quadrants. During this time, Ms. Valentine slunk down the aisle four times, each time yelling a new command: "Razor!" "Blunt cutting!" "Effilating!" "Thinning shears!" This was not creating an environment in which I felt I could do my best work.

Upon looking at the clock I realized that I had only three minutes left; it was with a great sense of urgency that I launched into my excess-bulk removal and shaping.

In the twenty minutes given for the permanent waving segment of the exam, I resectioned the hair and then, using wee, slippery pieces of tissue paper, put about one third of it up in curlers. At the conclusion of the segment, Ms. Valentine announced that we would break for lunch. Some ten seconds later four girls had swarmed around the wig dryer out of which they stealthily pulled the Tupperware containers full of chop suey and rice and beans that would serve as their lunches.

After lunch we fingerwaved. According to Ms. Valentine, fingerwaving—the process by which one molds hair into even, 1930s-style ridges—is the most difficult part of the exam; "Sometimes students just break down crying during it." She gave me a plastic bottle of fingerwaving lotion—a sticky, viscous substance evocative of whipped spit. I labored diligently during this twenty-minute leg of the exam; although I was unable to create the plates and ridges of hair with which the other students were transforming their heads into what looked like well-lubricated armadillos, I *was* able to create a mottled, wavy look that had its own eerie beauty.

At the conclusion of testing, I asked to see my exam scoresheet. Ms. Valentine smiled bleakly and slightly maternally. Next to where she had written that I had garnered a thirty out of a possible fifty on the comb-out, was written "too fluffy" and "removed by brushing"; next to my thirty out of a possible fifty on the hair shaping, she had written "poor." She had not even bothered to score the permanent waving or fingerwaving sections.

"So I'm not ready for my own salon," I said.

"The comb-out was the only part that was close to passing."

"Yes, I felt good about that part," I said. "But will someone hire me if I can only do comb-outs?"

"Don't worry—you will not be hired soon."

"Maybe I could specialize. Maybe I could just do comb-ou—"

Ms. Valentine extolled the virtues of a proper Wilfred training; I thanked her for her guidance and left.

SO YOU WANT TO BE A SCENIC ARTIST

The painter of theatrical scenery who is interested in gaining admittance into Local 829, the United Scenic Artists, fits into one of two categories: Track A is for scenic artists with two or more years of professional experience; Track B is for people with "more traditional design and/or painting skills." Deciding that my own painting history is "more traditional," I applied for the latter. No résumé, letter of recommendation, interview, or portfolio is required for Track B admission into the union; one must simply pay $150, successfully complete a Home Project, and pass a studio painting test.

One month before the painting test, I was mailed two 8″ × 10″ color reproductions of paintings: the Home Project. I painted larger versions (3′ 9″ × 5′ 2″ and 4′ 6″ × 6′ 0″) of the two reproductions onto cotton duck. This year's paintings were "Drapery, Molding, Marble, Wood," a picture of a marble-arched wooden door on top of which someone has carelessly draped a lot of striped fabric, and "Still Life," a picture of a typical cliffside picnic.

On the Saturday morning of the eight-hour painting test I arrived at the basement of the ABC/Capital Cities studio at West End Avenue and Sixty-sixth Street at eight-thirty A.M. I stacked my rolled-up paintings on top of the other candidates' work at the entryway. Inside the studio the test's organizers had marked out some forty-five 5′ ½″ × 4′ ⅞″ painting areas on long rolls of muslin spread out and stapled to the floor. I picked a spot and unloaded my supplies. The other candidates, most of whom were in their twenties or thirties, were hunched over their areas of canvas, applying grids. Just before nine we gathered round, and one of the union members gave us a short speech in which she welcomed us to the Track B exam, told us to "relax and enjoy" ourselves, but explained that if we didn't stop painting at five P.M., one of the test's organizers would take the paintbrush from our hands. There were three palettes of paint for our use—Muralo, Iddings casein, and Rosco Super Saturated acrylic; the paints were located in some fifty plastic buckets at the far end of the studio.

When we returned to the work area, we each had a sealed manila envelope lying on our canvas. Upon opening their envelopes to reveal lovely prints of a watercolor goldfish, most of the candidates started to frantically complete their gridding, some of them using plumb lines and one using a clear plastic sheet with gridding on it, which he taped on top of his watercolor. Others of us relied on rulers and yardsticks, calmly reasserting the "more traditional" up-bringing.

After I had gridded my own muslin, I walked over to the paint area and filled nine small plastic containers with paint. As I was carrying four of these back to my work area, a male candidate in glasses and a gray workshirt came up beside me. His self-confidence was nervous-making.

"I see you're using the Muralo," he said.

"Yes," I said, slightly defensively.

"How come?"

I had chosen Muralo because there had been fewer peo-ple in line for it. But I did not want to reveal this to this man.

"I, unh . . . I like a paint with a little *spank factor* in it," I said.

This confused the man and he went away.

As I painted, I found it difficult to capture the gauzy effects of watercolor. The man to my left, a Russian, was getting wonderful results with many thin washes of color. I emulated his style with some success.

At one-ten, although no one else seemed to be eating, I squatted at the bottom of my workspace and ate the lunch that the union's guidelines had suggested I bring. I chose not to conclude my meal with any of the Oreos or Pecan Sandies that the local had provided, loath as I am to eat anything served by someone who has just opened and stirred several hundred gallons of paint.

At about four-ten I decided to chat up one of the organizers. He told me that the work of this year's group of candidates was *much* better than last year's.

"I'm crazy about *this* guy's work," I whispered, pointing to the Russian.

"Yes, it's nice," he offered.

"*Very* Track A," I said. "My work feels . . . *flat* to me. It, it doesn't quite come up off the canvas."

"Yes," he said, warily. "You lost some of the water effects you had going. If it'd been me, I would've avoided *everything* but the Super Saturates."

"How come?" I asked.

"The undercolor doesn't work up on you."

I nodded in agreement.

I resumed painting.

At the end of the exam, I spoke to a smiley organizer.

"Do you like mine?" I asked.

"Yes, you did a nice job," she said.

"Everyone else's is much better than mine."

"No, you did fine."

"I have problems with undercolors," I confided. "I have an undercolor problem."

"Well, if you fail the test you can always take it again," she said.

"You, unh, do you think I'll fail?"

"I can't tell you that," she said warmly.

Three days later I received a form letter telling me that I had failed and that I could schedule a review of my work for the fall. There was no mention made of an undercolor problem.

SO YOU WANT TO BE A MACY'S SALESPERSON

On a lovely, balmy spring day, I went to Macy's and applied for a sales job. After receiving a pass from a guard stationed at the entryway to the employees-only part of the store, I walked down several long corridors to personnel. Upon arriving at the personnel desk, I was handed an application attached to a clipboard and told to have a seat and fill the application out.

I jotted down my particulars, claiming to have done a lot of catering and to have been a salesperson for four years at someplace called the Brookfield Shop in West Brookfield, Massachusetts. Upon doing this, I noticed that the application asked, "What businesses, jobs, or professions do you know about from having a close friend or relative who worked in them?" Anticipating what kind of answer would endear me to the personnel people, I instantly thought of my sister, and wrote down "Nurse." Then, when asked to elaborate upon what the best features of that job were, I simply jotted down "Helping people get better"; when asked what the worst features were, I wrote, "Watching people die."

In response to "What are the most important things that make a company a good place to work?" and "What are some things you didn't like about jobs you've had?" I made obsequious comments about "effective communication between workers and management," "opportunity for advancement," "too much downtime" and the like.

The personable young woman who took my application from me gave it a cursory glance to make sure that I had filled everything out. Then, smiling, she asked if I had time to fill out another form. I readily obliged.

The second form was a booklet with some forty multiple-choice and true-false questions about my personality and behavior. Although I tried my best to divine what qualities are sought in a Macy's employee, it was not always easy to know how to respond to the questions. I answered in the affirmative to "Do you shop here often?" and responded "true" to "As a child I was always the one who tried to keep the class quiet when the teacher left the room." However, when posed "Do you always follow your orders quickly and cheerfully?" and "If there is no one else around to notice what you are doing, do you always pick up the paper and trash others leave around?" I answered no, fearful that I might seem irksome or fascistic. I tried to add a dash of moral probity to my personality profile by answering "true" to "It bothers me when a smart lawyer uses the law to get a criminal off." Given that the successful completion of this questionnaire would, I assumed, lead to an interview with a member of the personnel staff, I was somewhat surprised by the question "When interviewing for a job, how much difficulty do you experience in talking to the interviewer?" Wouldn't the person interviewing me be able to answer this for him or herself? I could only imagine that the personnel staff is so busy picking up the paper and trash that others leave behind that they are unable to focus on this issue.

The statement that proved the most difficult to respond to was a statement of the "Have you stopped beating your wife yet?" variety: "If I had had a fair chance in life, I would have been more successful." Given that I feel that I *have* had a fair chance in life, there is no way for me to answer this. I sat and thought about how I would answer variants of the statement—if I had had a less fair chance than I had, I might be less successful; if I had had a fairer chance than I had, I probably wouldn't be applying for a job at Macy's—but I was stymied by the question in its present redaction. My inability to answer began to gnaw at my self-confidence. I impulsively circled "false."

When I handed in my booklet and answer sheet, the woman who took them from me thanked me and told me that someone would call soon. But I did not receive a phone call. Two months later I called the personnel department and was told that applications are only good for thirty days and that I should reapply. "We'll be needing more people for Mother's Day," the woman whom I spoke to told me.

Upon returning, I filled out a second application in much the way I had before. The chief difference was, when queried again about jobs that I was familiar with, I thought of my *other* sister, and wrote "Primate Center Manager." When asked what the best features of the job were, I wrote, "Overseeing staff, organizing events"; when asked what the worst features were, I wrote, "Seeing chimps die."

I was not asked to take a personality test. I did not receive a phone call.

SO YOU WANT TO BE A DOG GROOMER

How do you prepare a cocker spaniel for being taken to the Holiday Inn at the Newark airport in order to be groomed for the National Dog Groomers Association of America's certification test?

There is no way, I decided. The only thing for me to do was to try to acclimate the dog to the potential vagaries of the nonprofessional grooming experience by inviting the little fellow to pass a night in my home. I called Clifford's owner and arranged to pick him up the night before the testing.

Clifford is not inconvenienced by the limitations of tact; he is a paunchy five-year-old who has heartworms and who mistakes irritability for personality. Imagine Broderick Crawford on all fours, in an ill-fitting suit. I could not allow his reputation for having bitten several people in the past to dissuade me from deciding to work with him; suffice it to say that the response to my search for a dog had not been overwhelming. That his owner has no pretensions to Clifford's being a show dog made the prospect of using him all the more attractive. Clifford was the natural choice: he had the required eight weeks, if not more, of unimpeded hair growth.

Upon arriving at my building, however, he immediately established what kind of houseguest he would be. He would not climb my stairs until jerked. He bid an upturned snout to the kibble and other savory treats offered him. He

would not allow me to effilate his groin area. I did not want
to press my luck with him; the more I looked over the
guidelines and Breed Profiles that the NDGAA had sent
me—"It is advisable when testing," one read, "to try and
use a dog not sensitive to burns, so you can clip clean and
close"—the more anxious I became. Indeed, when it became clear after walking him that night that Clifford's paws
required washing, I prevailed upon my boyfriend Jess to
lower this unpleasant battleship into the harbor of my bathtub.

Clifford spent much of the evening barking at my refrigerator. We awoke bleary-eyed the next morning at five
forty-five and drove to the Holiday Inn Jetport. Going
inside and confirming with the two judges that I was the
owner of a Greenwich Village dog salon called Ruff Trade,
I registered myself while Jess encouraged an increasingly
vexed Clifford to urinate in the parking lot. The testing was
being conducted in the Frank Borman Room; chairs had
been stacked on the side, and large sheets of plastic had
been taped to the carpeting. Two female groomers dressed
in smocky, pastel groomwear had set up their tables and
were talking to their uncaged dogs; I set up my table next
to a power-pak, into which one of the women encouraged
me to "plug-in." When I saw that the other woman's dog
was a cocker spaniel whose hair was far more fluffy and
lustrous than Clifford's, I nervously helped Jess guide the
addled Clifford into the adjacent Chuck Yeager Room for
a last-minute comb-out.

Several minutes later we took Clifford into the testing

room and eased him onto the grooming table just as the younger judge began circling the room with a clipboard to inspect each of the nine dogs. After putting her nose up to Clifford's side and inhaling, she palpated his ears. Clifford grumbled ominously. "Your dog has mats," she said. It was true; I had neglected to brush them out the evening before. "That's part of my grooming process," I explained to the woman. She wrote a note on her clipboard.

Seconds later she announced the commencement of grooming. The room whirred to life with the buzzing of electric clippers. I took my clippers and, running them along Clifford's side and back, discovered that this was not entirely pleasurable to him. He growled loudly, causing one of the other groomers to look over at us with concern. The Breed Profile for the cocker spaniel advises that one closely trim "the folds in the lower jaw area (flews), where the hair is apt to hold saliva"; I considered doing this, but decided that I was not anxious to see Clifford's reaction to my applying electricity to his saliva. Falling back on my cosmetological training, I took out my flame-tempered #10 shears and began to reduce some of the excess bulk on Clifford's legs. When I proceeded with this activity on and around his stomach, he began to make a low-pitched rumbling sound reminiscent of large aircraft. For reasons unclear to me even now, I then decided that this was the time to work on Clifford's mats. Picking up my comb, I lifted his left ear. But upon my touching said comb to the hair behind his ear, Clifford snarled and lifted his left lip, revealing a glistening incisor.

This behavior was distressing to me—as it would be, I'm sure, to any groomer. There seemed to be little that Clifford was going to allow me to do to him; surely I would fail the test if my dog exhibited no change in his appearance. Fortunately, I had had the presence of mind to bring along a few extra supplies; it was thus with a sense of professional ardor that, clamping Clifford's mouth shut with one hand, I pulled a lipstick from my bag with the other and proceeded to smear my snarly friend's snout with Clinique Citrus Pink. When I saw that the top third of the other cocker spaniel's ears were being clipped so unattractively "clean and close" that you could see the veins and skin underneath, I applied a generous daub of alcohol-free Dep styling gel to Clifford's left ear and then curled several of its long tufts of hair on his ear up into a curler. Waiting for this to set, I applied two liberal coats of Hai Karate cologne to his back and midsection.

My nontraditional grooming methods were at first almost wholly uninteresting to the judges and other groomers, four of whom were having a passionate discussion about bringing one's children along on the dog and cat show circuits.

"That's the only thing about cat cages," said one woman. "You can't fit a kid in there."

"*Bet* me," another countered. "*Bet* me. My friend Marie has a Siamese and she tours constantly and I've seen her put her kid in one. *Easy.*"

At the conclusion of the hour-and-a-half exam period, the younger of the two judges picked up her clipboard and made her way over to Clifford and me. Silently she ran my comb through Clifford's hair. She lifted his right ear. She lifted his left ear.

"You hardly cut any of his hair," she said.

"I know," I responded. "This is what I call a Lite Groom."

She looked at me suspiciously. Then she went back to the older judge and whispered in her ear. The older judge was a muscular, compact woman who seemed to be perpetually on the boil. She walked over to us looking like a woman with a mission. After raking my comb through Clifford's right hindquarter, she said in a forceful tone, "This is totally unacceptable."

"Oh," I said, somewhat forlornly. "What about the ears? I was trying to get some *volume* with his ears."

"Not with mats you don't!" she said. She continued to look him over, wincing as she fully beheld the lipstick.

"I unh . . . I was trying to capture a sense of the unexpected," I offered.

"No, I'm sorry, this dog is not acceptable. You should familiarize yourself with our Breed Profiles." She looked again at the Citrus Pink.

"It's lipstick," I said. "It's my grooming signature. I like a dog with a *face*."

She exhaled loudly and laid my comb down on my table next to one of the curlers. She explained that I had failed the practical part of the test but that I could take the written part.

I put Clifford and my supplies in the car and then re-

turned to the testing room. The written test consisted of
twenty-nine true or false questions and thirty-two outlines
of dogs to be identified by breed. The older judge corrected
my test while I waited, telling me I got a 56 percent on the
written and 0 percent on the practical. The written critique
of my practical work included the comment "Dog smells
doggy." I declined to point out that this was unlikely since
the dog was wearing a nationally distributed men's cologne.
Both the critique and the older judge encouraged me to
review the association's Breed Profiles and to attend more
dog shows.

We drove home in silence.

SO YOU WANT TO BE A CEMENT MASON

Having mailed in an application in which I claimed to have
the required "three years of full-time satisfactory experience
as a cement mason, plus sufficient full-time satisfactory
experience as a mason's helper," I walked to Seward Park
High School on Grand Street one Saturday morning to take
the written civil-service test for cement masons. About two
hundred men were already waiting in line when I got there.

"It's all who you know," said the man standing in line
behind me about the difficulty of getting work as a mason.
"It's all Mob. Completely Mob-run."

I did not pursue this line of conversation, surrounded as
we were by large Italian men.

The test consisted of eighty questions, almost all of them

specific to the trade. I did not know what screeding is. I did not know what the proper tool for preventing honeycombing is. When asked "Which two of these tools have the most similar purposes: a) strike-off rod and bull flat b) edger and jitterbug c) bull float and darby d) groover and darby," the tools all sounded to me like dance steps of the thirties and forties; however, my subsequent search for mentions of the Trunky-Doo was completely in vain.

Ever since I took this test, I have spent more time thinking about sidewalks.

SO YOU WANT TO BE A PSYCHIC

When my friend B.W. returned from Miami one day and told me that he had read about an organization that certifies psychics, something about his calm and assured tone made me think that my vocational ship might finally have come in. I called the Florida phone number he gave me and spoke to an employee of the Universal Centre in Cassadaga. A New Age seminarium with an extensive metaphysical bookstore, the Centre has three psychic readers who are available from ten A.M. to five P.M. every day on the premises or from ten A.M. to four-thirty P.M. over the phone (MasterCard, VISA, and American Express accepted). But the woman whom I spoke to knew nothing about certification; she said that the man who was in charge of it was Dr. Sekunna, the founder of the Centre. She gave me his phone number.

I told Dr. Sekunna that I was a psychic who had been

giving readings for seven years. He explained to me that people interested in becoming readers at the Centre must give an accurate reading for either Dr. Sekunna or one of the other Centre members; upon successful completion, the candidates "work with" and train under Dr. Sekunna for a period of months or even years.

I asked Dr. Sekunna if I could give him a reading over the phone.

"Sure," he said.

I paused dramatically.

"Orange," I said. "It's a, it's a color that has become important to you. It was not until very recently."

"That's true. Orange is to me a very earth color. It's an earth spiritual color. You'll find that a lot of Eastern mystics and yogis use the color orange in their spiritual work. In the past few years I've been very attracted to the color orange as a very spiritual color. If I was going to wear a robe, it would be orange."

"I'm seeing a little man with a beard who is living not in the hollow of a tree, but very close. He's very in touch with the woods. He is a sort of modern leprechaun. He has bells on his shoes."

"I'll try to explain that one to you," Dr. Sekunna said, as he began to tell me about a Centre member who had moved from Miami to the more rural Cassadaga area. "You look at this guy and you want to call him a leprechaun. He's got an impish type of personality."

I was warming to this endeavor.

"I'm sensing . . . I'm sensing *cheese,*" I intoned. "I'm

not sure if it's a Roquefort or something from the Pyre-
nees—but it's some kind of *blue cheese.*"

"Well, I enjoy all kinds of cheeses," he explained. "It's
what I think I shouldn't eat so much of."

"That's no doubt where it's coming from," I explained
matter-of-factly. "I'm also sensing that the underside of
tables is perhaps something that fascinates you."

"The underside of tables?"

"Yes, the underside of things," I continued calmly.
"From a *dog's* perspective."

This seemed to give him pause. But then, finally: "Yes,
I'm an investigator in life. I like to see what's on the bottom
as well as what's on the top."

When I had finished my reading, Dr. Sekunna said I was
"very highly sensitive." He gave me the name of a numerology book that espouses a simpler, "more spiritual" approach to numerology than most; although I have "an
affinity with numbers," he felt that I "get annoyed by
numbers" and that when I was studying math as a child, I
probably felt that what was being taught me was incorrect.

Twelve days later Dr. Sekunna unexpectedly called me
back. Saying he had been looking over my chart, he tried to
encourage me to go to Florida and take five hours of
palmistry lessons with him for one hundred dollars. If those
went well, I would then continue training for "a month or
two."

"The more I've been thinking about you, the more I
realize you're a touch person," he said. "If we worked on
that sensitivity that you already have, and then add palmistry

skills, we have the ability to have you make four or five hundred dollars a week."

"So you, you think I'm a touch person," I said.

"You *are* a touch person!"

"I've always wondered."

"Absolutely. You're a touch person."

Having asked me if I am "locked in to New York," he then explained that he hoped to open another Centre within a couple of months.

"This is exciting," I said. "And you think potentially you see me at this new Centre or do you think maybe there would be a spot opening at the current Centre?"

"I'll have a slot for you one way or the other."

Call me psychic.

WHAT IF A JURY WERE SEQUESTERED AT CAESARS PALACE?

Voir Dire	Lawyer tries to intimidate juror with Latin phrase *Circus Maximus.*
Oath	Jurors pledge oath that they will not reveal finale of *Boylesque.*
Trial	Daydreaming juror considers alternate career as Caesars Palace wine goddess.
Recess	Juror adorns statue of Justice outside courthouse with gold lamé loincloth.
Sequestration	Juror flooded with reasonable doubt during overture to *Nudes on Ice.*
Sequestration	Bailiff elopes with waitress who is dressed as Cleopatra.
Verdict	Foreman announces, "Ladies and gentlemen, you have been a very special gallery."

WHAT IF THE U.S. GOVERNMENT WERE RUN BY TEENAGE GIRLS?

Monday   President tells Pentagon official, "Fragrance is the ultimate body language."

Tuesday   Speaker of the House sees Republicans passing note; humiliates junior senator by forcing her to read note aloud to joint session of Congress.

Wednesday   Chief of staff slashes wrists in White House bathroom.

Thursday   Vice president rushes off to Kennedy Center: first after-work meeting for *Oklahoma!* costume committee.

Friday   President assigns numerical value to each letter in alphabet to predict numerologically whether recent legislation will be successful.

Saturday   Secretary of state retreats to Georgetown home to curl up with clove cigarettes and *The Bell Jar.*

Sunday   Commander in chief accidentally signs nuclear arms treaty "Mrs. Matthew Broderick."

WHAT IF PHIL DONAHUE ERUPTED
INTO FLAMES?

4:07 P.M. Producers of *Oprah* decide to lower Oprah into jaws of shark.

4:18 P.M. Marlo expresses relief that Phil's insides are not lumber.

4:27 P.M. Woman in audience recounts unrelated personal anecdote.

4:42 P.M. Woman in audience recounts unrelated personal anecdote.

4:53 P.M. Woman in audience recounts unrelated personal anecdote.

Nackt Tonight, Darling

HYPOTHESIS: Possessed as I am of an endless fascination with the classified advertising sections of small newspapers, I often come across ads placed by nude housecleaners. Such a profession, it has always seemed, must be slightly . . . *imperiling.* Standing in the altogether while scouring a recalcitrant stovetop; wrangling ungarmented with a chunk of ice lodged in a winterscape of spilled Frogurt—these are chores fraught with occupational hazard. And, although nudism has a history rife with discipline and rigor—nudism as a philosophy started early in this century in Germany, where the *Nacktkultur* (meaning naked culture) movement prescribed calisthenics, medicinal baths, diets, and purges as the means toward spiritual equanimity and biological purity—I have always imagined the contemporary urban nudist to be an individual of slightly less gusto.

EXPERIMENT: In an attempt to test the mettle of the nude domestic, I conducted a small experiment. On two separate occasions I called a nude housecleaning service and hired cleaners—one man, one woman—to come to my home (sixty dollars an hour, with a two-hour minimum). In addition to having these cleaners perform traditional duties like sweeping and dusting, I asked them to complete tasks that I thought might prove especially challenging to those in nature's garb.

But before we turn to the data, allow me to say that both cleaners were kind, unintimidating people, neither of whom was interested in rendering me pants-less. Indeed, chief among my initial curiosities had been whether or not nude housecleaning is a euphemism for prostitution; both cleaners assured me it is not.

"The visual is okay," one of them explained to me, "but it's a hands-off policy."

DATA: I knew little about these people before they came to my home and shucked their clothing; they knew nothing about me except my name and address. I was told by the service that the first cleaner, a man, was *"very big* in all areas" (and thus, for the purpose of this report, I shall refer to him as Big); when I called to hire a second cleaner, I asked for a woman with a "fun personality" (and thus, for the purpose of this report, I shall refer to her as Fun).

"Die Vinder" (Windows)

TASK: Clean blinds-less windows looking onto busy residential street

POTENTIAL OCCUPATIONAL HAZARD: Public exposure; arrest

RESULTS:

Big: "I don't usually do windows, but it's spring and you should really be able to see out them." When told that windows had no blinds: "I don't mind. I mean, hey— *you* live here." Used newspaper and Fantastik; seemed to relish parts of task. Readjusted athletic socks throughout.

Fun, upon seeing windows: "Oh my God! Can people see me? Where are your shades?" Later, in kitchen, when asked if she'd be willing to clean windows: "Windows? I've never done windows." Did not do windows.

"Das Stoop und Grope" (Low, Hard-to-Reach Places)

TASK: Bend and stoop in order to dust low, hard-to-reach area located two and a half feet under antique desk

POTENTIAL OCCUPATIONAL HAZARD: Possible prominent display of unattractive body part

RESULTS: Both cleaners immediately got down on hands and knees, their preferred cleaning position; both deftly angled body so as to avoid aforementioned display.

Big: was particularly impressed by desk; *"That's* a nice

piece." Extolled virtues of Goddard's furniture polish—
"It won't build up like other polishes do." Volunteered
to make list of cleaning supplies necessary for gracious
living.

Fun: chatty throughout.

"Das Newspapperschmutz" (Newsprint)

TASK: Carry twenty-inch bundle of newspapers a thirty-
five-foot distance

POTENTIAL OCCUPATIONAL HAZARD: Bodily besmirchment

RESULTS: Both eluded blemishing by breaking pile down
into three loads and carrying loads out in front of body.

Big: "Do you have any twine? I can even bundle them for
you." Paid especial attention to papers' subsequent
placement. Renewed offer to make list of cleaning supplies necessary for gracious living.

Fun: "This is a lot of papers." Brief conversation about
comic-strip character Cathy.

"Die Gluetrappen" (Glue Traps)

TASK: Set glue traps in hard-to-reach location

POTENTIAL OCCUPATIONAL HAZARD: Unpleasantness arising as a result of extremity getting caught in glue

RESULTS: Both circumvented ensnarement.

Big: completed task with removal of athletic socks.

Fun: "I step in these things all the time."

Me: "When you're nude?"

Fun: "No, at home. I drag them all over the house. My nieces love this."

"Die Fireloggen" (Firewood)

TASK: Carry bundle of firewood a thirty-five-foot distance

POTENTIAL OCCUPATIONAL HAZARD: Splinters

RESULTS: Both efficiently carried the six halved logs that I had borrowed from a friend. Neither received splinters; neither mentioned that I do not have a fireplace.

Big: resembled human andiron.

Fun: "Wood is not so heavy."

"Acid in Tub" (Acid in Tub)

TASK: Unclog bathtub drain with Hot Spot, a professional-strength drain opener containing concentrated sulfuric acid

POTENTIAL OCCUPATIONAL HAZARD: Fonduelike death throes

RESULTS: Both cleaners were highly excited by my squat, deep tub. Big said, "It'd be good for groups—good for a party," and Fun enthused, "Look at this tub! You could really drown in it! I've gotta get myself one of these." They were less excited, however, about the acid.

Big: "I'll use it, but you should really just use bleach once a month. It won't eat through your pipes."

Fun: "Sulfuric acid? Are you crazy? This is for plumbers—I mean, this could splash in your face and make you very ugly!" Upon being told that she only needed to pour out an inch of the acid, Fun calmed down and completed the task. She poured the acid splashlessly; she does not now resemble a plumber.

CONCLUSION: My data do not support my hypothesis. With the exception of Fun's refusal to do windows, the cleaners' work was thorough and efficient. My exacting standards were met repeatedly (as was my suspicion that my visits from naked strangers might have their more awkward moments—Big, while dusting under the couch I was sitting on, at one point playfully lifted my foot up, dusted underneath it, and then let it thud to the ground; Fun, while embarking on a half-hour degrouting of my bathtub tile, asked, "Do you mind if, while I'm cleaning the bathroom, I *use* the bathroom?").

Nevertheless, I can now rest assured that, in homes throughout New York City and the state of California, domestics are busily and capably defrosting freezers, recycling rusty cans, and sharpening knives—all without the benefit of a protective layer of clothing.

Heil Nacktkultur.

WHAT IF SIGMUND FREUD HAD BEEN
A FORMER FASHION MODEL?

1894   Freud dubs new patient "Frau K." due to his inability to remember other letters in her name.

1895   Freud tries to shock colleague with confession that he was an ugly, gawky teenager.

1901   Freud disappoints Viennese intellectuals when his long-awaited "book" consists of nothing but photos of Freud pouting vacantly.

1907   Freud tells young trainee, "Catalogue work—that's your bread and butter."

1912   Jung and Adler break away from Freud, claiming he overemphasizes the importance of runway.

1914   Freud's impassioned speech to Vienna Psychoanalytical Society finds members murmuring, "Who is Coco?"

1915   Scholars reveal that *Dora: An Analysis of a Case of Hysteria* is actually about an agent at Zoli.

WHAT IF A GROUP OF PLASTIC SURGEONS STARTED PUBLISHING AN OBSCURE LITERARY JOURNAL CALLED *CONTOURS?*

Monday Fiction editor hires former patient to be assistant; introduces her to staff as "one of my rhinos."

Tuesday Contributor submits poem, "Gauzy Revelation."

Wednesday Publisher suggests that contributors' notes include "before" Polaroids.

Thursday Withdrawal of investor necessitates loss of five pages; editor announces he will "vacuum" the Sontag story.

Friday Art director borders all pages with black edging; likens effect to permanent lashlining.

Saturday Contributor submits memoir, "Low-Bleed Implants I Have Known."

Sunday Editor signs off on first issue; drives to Yaddo; slips into foam post-op girdle.

WHAT IF THE POPE WERE A DOG?

Monday   Pope rejects surplice and miter regalia; opts for simple leather collar.

Tuesday   Pope replaces ritual of "washing the feet of the poor" with licking the faces of the recently fed.

Wednesday   Pope photographed in embarrassing moment of physiological necessity when he mistakes member of Swiss Guard for yet more St. Peter's statuary.

Thursday   Pope requests meeting with actress June Lockhart.

Friday   Pope follows foreign dignitary's request to "please be seated" with demand for unspecified "treat."

Saturday   World Council of Churches meeting delayed when Pope's scratching of his belly's "skritchy spot" causes his inactive left leg to flail wildly.

Sunday   Pope attacks recently delivered newspaper; gets rubber band stuck on nose.

Drive, He Said

I have long desired to be a part of "the process." As George Bush wrote in his autobiography, *Looking Forward*, "Anything that brings the process closer to the people is all to the good"; as Tom Hayden said to Bryant Gumbel several years ago, "The process today gives everyone a chance to participate." If two minds as divergent as those of Mr. Bush and Mr. Hayden could agree on an issue, I decided, then the issue bears examination.

So when a friend called me to tell me that she had volunteered to drive VIPs to their various duties during the 1992 Democratic National Convention, I did not allow my lack of automotive brio to dissuade me from entering the fray.

Yes, I say lack of automotive brio. You see, I do not own a car; I have never owned a car. To own a car in New York, it seems, would be to fly in the face of necessity, economy, and convenience—an act tantamount to bringing a sandwich to a restaurant. Consequently, the confidence that I might have about my driving were I to do it more frequently is sorely lacking; those rare occasions when I *do* find myself behind the wheel in a metropolitan area are marked by cautiousness and a sense of impending peril. I sit very, very close to the steering wheel; indeed, in the best of all possible driving worlds, I would be seated *on* the steering wheel.

These facts notwithstanding, I called the phone number for volunteer drivers and was granted an appointment for an interview.

=

Two weeks later, in a makeshift midtown office overrun with Democrats, I wrote my name, address, phone number, and desired position ("VIP driver") on a form, whereupon a gaunt man in his sixties brought me into his office.

"Know your way around the city?" he asked me.

"Sure."

"Drive much around the city?"

"No," I confessed. "Not really."

"Well, it really doesn't matter. As long as you know midtown, it's mostly that."

He then asked me for my driver's license, explaining that he was going to Xerox it.

"You have any moving violations?" he asked matter-of-factly.

"No."

"We'll find out if you do, so it doesn't matter."

He then posed a hypothetical situation: He was a delegate who, at two o'clock on a sunny day, was exiting Madison Square Garden (where the Democratic Convention was to be held) and had one hour to see some sights. Where would I take him?

Thinking how my stepfather, when in New York, likes to go to jazz clubs in order to "listen to some sounds," I told the man that I would drive down Seventh Avenue and point out the Village Vanguard to him.

"Maybe you like jazz," I explained.

His expression suggested that he did not like jazz.

I then suggested that we continue down Seventh Avenue and make our way down to the financial district.

". . . If you have time," he cut me off. "Then you could see the Statue of Liberty and all that crap."

Although it was not my intention to gain access to political dignitaries so that I might expose them to "crap," I nodded my head so as to suggest that I am a team player.

After Xeroxing my license, the man took me to a small conference room where Ron Coleman, the Motorpool manager, was talking to small groups of applicants. On a form that listed the four days of the convention plus the weekends before and after it, I indicated that I was available on a full-time basis for all ten days. Upon exiting the conference room, I realized that I wasn't sure if I had been hired or not.

"So I'll hear from you?" I asked Mr. Coleman. "I mean, is there a test we have to take or anything?"

"No, no, you're in!" he said. "We need everyone we can get. You'll hear from us next week with an assignment."

I was startled by the ease with which I had been hired. No one had asked me my occupation. No one had administered a driving test. No one had tested my ability to lean on a horn and spew obscenities in Afghani.

=

Eight days later, at a meeting attended by some two hundred drivers, the ground plans were laid out: General Motors would be lending both the Democratic Convention and the Republican Convention 175 sedans and minivans. The DNC had comprehensive insurance coverage with $1 million liability for each accident, but drivers were responsible for all moving and parking violations. Overnight parking at Meyers Garage on Thirty-fourth Street would be paid for by the DNC upon the driver's showing his parking card; short-term parking would be paid for by the VIPs.

One of the speakers at the meeting was a short, mustachioed detective from the New York Police Department who, in a discussion of safety measures, cautioned us to be sensitive to something that he referred to as "the uh-oh feeling."

"Listen to your gut instincts," he said. "That 'uh-oh feeling'? *Listen to it.*"

=

Five days later I went to the Motorpool office and met with a well-dressed woman in her early twenties who was going to give me my assignment. Looking at a clipboard, she asked me, "What do you know about Colorado?"

"I've been there," I said. "I've never lived there."

"Hold on," she said, as she stood and left the room for some three minutes. Was she going to produce Colorado representative Pat Schroeder from the adjoining room? Would John Denver emerge looking for a ride to the Village? Was this the uh-oh feeling?

The young woman finally returned unaccompanied and said, "The guy who's about to come through the door is Ron Coleman, who's in charge of transportation."

Mr. Coleman came through the door and gushed, "Brian!"

"It's Henry," I said.

"Henry!"

"We're thinking of matching you with the governor of Colorado," the young woman said.

"Governor Romer," Mr. Coleman explained.

After the young woman had called me the next day and given me the governor's arrival time at LaGuardia the following Saturday, I did a little research. I discovered that the highly popular, twice-elected, sixty-three-year-old governor had a reputation for being unbridled. After reporters and news crews were dismissed from a meeting between President Bush and the country's governors in February 1992, Romer broke protocol by insisting that the press be allowed to stay to hear Democratic rebuttal to the president's budget and domestic policy proposals. Afterward, White House press secretary Marlin Fitzwater told *The Washington Post* that "the easiest, cheapest trick in the world is to be rude to the President to try to get into the news"; *The New York Times* later referred to the governor as "brash" and "unvarnished."

This information suggested only one thing to me: I would not be spending the convention singing rounds of *"Frère Jacques."*

SATURDAY

On Saturday morning I went to the motorpool office to pick up the keys, whereupon I was introduced to the governor's assistant campaign manager, Joan Coplan. An employee of the political consultant firm Stratton, Reiter, Dupree, and Durante, Miss Coplan is a short, take-charge woman, probably in her late thirties. She has a flat, Midwestern voice whose dial is permanently set on Resounding. We walked together to the garage and picked up our brand-new black Oldsmobile Ninety-Eight.

As Miss Coplan and I got to know one another on our way to the airport, the questions that she asked me suggested that she was expecting a driver of a more professional stripe: She asked if I drive in New York (I blithely told her, "No one does, really"); she asked, "So you've never had a car in the city before?"; she asked if I had a beeper. I started to feel more and more unsure of myself; surely these were the glimmerings of the uh-oh feeling. Indeed, when Miss Coplan went to make some phone calls in the airport waiting area, I thought that my career in politics might be rapidly drawing to a close.

However, no termination of my services was mentioned. Minutes later, the plane arrived. The first member of the Romer group to step off the plane was the governor's chief of staff, B. J. Thornberry, a warm, attractive, cherubic woman in her forties graced with bright red cheeks and an air of savvy professionalism. When I had divested her of the air travel bag that had been slung over her shoulder, I turned to find the governor looking at me with a slightly pained expression. I introduced myself first to him and then to his wife, who Miss Coplan had told me would spend most of the convention with a bodyguard named Toby. Because the governor's entry in *Who's Who in America* concludes with the rather mysterious accolade "Order of Coif."—an accolade that I could only imagine means "Order of Coiffure"—my impulse at this relatively early stage in my employment was, of course, to study his hair. It seemed highly Order-worthy; it successfully toed the line between bounce and volume.

As we headed toward Manhattan, the governor asked me what I do for a living; I told him that I tutor English and write book reviews. When he then asked how I had "hooked up with" him and his staff, I explained that they were assigned me.

"I'm glad you were assigned, Governor," Miss Thornberry joked. "No one would have picked you."

After decanting the group into the New York Hilton where they were all staying, I parked the car in a garage across the street. Then, as I had been instructed to do each day, I called the man in Motorpool who was in charge of VIP arrangements.

"They seem pleased with you?" he asked me.

"Well I guess you'll hear from them if they're not."

"I have one tip for you," he said. "And don't take this as criticism. You're wearing a blue golf shirt?"

"I'm wearing a black golf shirt and a blue blazer."

"Right. So what you should do is look at how his aides are dressed. Then dress just like them."

"Really?"

"Yeah. Try to blend in with them as much as possible. It's *mirroring* them. That way, when they go out to dinner and stuff, there's more likelihood that they'll bring you along if you dress like them."

"Both his aides are women."

"Oh."

"Yeah."

"Well you can't wear a dress. But you know what I'm saying. Blend in. Look at what the governor is wearing."

"Right."

"Just trying to let you take advantage of one of the perks of the job."

I thanked him for his advice and hung up.

Miss Coplan had instructed me to have the car waiting in the rear carport of the Hilton at six forty-five. I got permission from one of the Hilton garage's attendants to leave the car in the loading zone for what he stipulated was to be "a few minutes." Miss Coplan arrived at six-fifty and said that if I was asked to move the car that I should "tell them it's Governor Romer."

Some fifteen minutes later I was whisking the governor and his two staff members off to a reception that *The Denver Post* was holding at the Water Club for the Colorado delegates. On the way, the governor asked me if I had had to take a driving test in order to volunteer at the convention.

"No," I confessed. "I'm very raw."

Indeed, the largely intuitive nature of my driving was born out half a block later when, driving at about thirty mph, I suddenly swerved to avoid a manhole that rose some six inches above the surface of Fifty-fourth Street between Sixth and Fifth avenues.

Miss Thornberry looked slightly alarmed. "You don't normally drive in the city, do you?" she asked.

"No," I responded. "No one does, really."

The governor's staff very graciously encouraged me to attend both functions that evening: the *Denver Post* party and the Democratic National Convention Welcoming Reception, held in the lobby of Grand Central Station. I was flattered and a little surprised to be included, particularly given that I hadn't been *mirroring*.

During the parties I tried to stay outside the governor's line of vision; given that he had said nothing when the misses Thornberry and Coplan had invited me to the events, I did not want to run the risk of my presence falling under the category of the Servant Problem. However, toward the conclusion of the DNC party, all four of us discovered that, independently of one another, we had drifted down to the far end of the room where the dessert table was located. Moments later the governor scanned my person and said, "You're thin. You should eat some desserts."

SUNDAY

The following morning, I picked the car up from the garage on Thirty-fourth Street where I had been instructed by the men in the Motorpool office to park. Upon meeting Miss Coplan at the appointed hour at the Hilton, I told her that, although the luxury of parking at the hotel itself had not been offered us by the men at the Motorpool office, it appeared that other members of the convention were doing it.

"If you ever need to park here," Miss Coplan said, "Just say 'Chairman Brown, Suite 4510.' "

Before I could give much thought to the possibility of charging our parking expenses to Ron Brown, the chairman of the Democratic National Committee, I was asked to take the governor and misses Coplan and Thornberry down to Madison Square Garden, where the governor was going to use the TelePrompTer to practice the speech he would give to the convention on Tuesday night.

I pulled up to the appointed unloading zone across from the Garden, a zone that was filled two-deep with limousines and cars. The governor and Miss Coplan got out of the car and slammed their doors, whereupon I suddenly realized that I had neglected to leave enough space for Miss Thornberry to open her door. She yelled, "I can't get out! I can't get out!" Flustered and embarrassed, I shifted the car into drive; but before I could ease away from the neighboring vehicle, she had slid across the seat and exited on the traffic side of the car.

In the late afternoon Miss Coplan introduced me to Rick Reiter of Stratton, Reiter, Dupree & Durante, who would be joining the entourage. Mr. Reiter appeared to be in his early forties and was composed of equal parts warm informality and boyish excitability.

I was starting to feel anxious about the governor's schedule for that evening. Each trip between the locations on his itinerary might, with traffic, take as long as half an hour. He wanted to leave the Hilton at four for a cocktail reception honoring House and Senate Democrats at the South Street Seaport; then to East Fiftieth Street for a five- to six-o'clock reception honoring Chairman Brown at the restaurant Tatou; back to the Seaport area from six-fifteen to seven for a party for the Coloradan and Hawaiian delegates; and then, most important, be at the Garden at seven-fifteen to give a live TV interview to *Crossroads*. I decided to ask someone's advice about this last and most daunting leg from the Seaport to the Garden; I went to the Motorpool office and talked to a volunteer driver in his sixties who claimed to have been driving in New York for thirty-five years. I asked him if I should take the fast-moving but inconveniently located FDR Drive or the conveniently located but slow-moving Church Street; he favored Church Street.

"Not the FDR?" I asked.

"No, Church," he said. But at the north end of Church Street, he cautioned, "You've got to get off on Sixth Avenue, then bear left and wiggle. You know what I mean by bear left and wiggle?"

I did not bear left and wiggle—as Diana Vreeland once observed, elegance is refusal. Instead, I took the FDR. By that point in the evening—my anxiety about our lateness to the preceding three events having caused my shoulders to rise so high as to suggest the gradual retraction of my neck—I longed for a direct, uncomplicated, unmediated expanse of thoroughfare. During the ride, the conversation between the governor and Mr. Reiter turned to the recent naming of Senator Albert Gore as Clinton's running mate.

"What do you think about the Gore announcement?" the governor asked Mr. Reiter.

"You know," Mr. Reiter said, "it plays better and better."

"It does play well."

Around eight-fifteen, the governor having gone back to the hotel earlier by cab, I drove Miss Coplan and Mr. Reiter to the Hilton from the Garden. On the way, Mr. Reiter, awed by the amount of congestion and activity in the streets, turned to me and exclaimed, "All this traffic. My God. How do you get by in New York?"

Miss Coplan explained, "He doesn't drive."

MONDAY

On Monday morning at seven-fifty, I positioned the car, as Mr. Reiter had instructed me the evening before, at the garage exit. Mr. Reiter came out of the hotel some five minutes later, whereupon we reviewed the day's schedule. Then he handed me a twenty-dollar bill and three ten-dollar bills.

"Here's some money to put in your pocket," he said. "You're gonna need it to bribe parking guys."

After Mr. Reiter had gone back into the hotel, I found myself staring at the dashboard, practicing saying the phrase, *Would Abraham Lincoln ease your worries, my friend?* It did not sound natural.

However, I was trying to be more aggressive on the road. On our way to the Waldorf-Astoria, where the governor was to attend a policy issues forum of the Democratic Governors' Association, I narrowly avoided disaster when I slipped the car in front of a bus in an attempt to get out of a slow-moving lane of traffic.

"Good move!" Mr. Reiter cheered.

The governor, in the backseat, said to Rick about me, "What I've decided about his driving is either that he's too young and green to know he's doing it, or he's a pro who's got it all figured out. I suspect the former."

Mr. Reiter recounted the specifics of an equally heart-stopping maneuver I had made with a bus the day before, saying, "I thought we were going to peel paint."

The governor added, "Yes, some of your clearances are amaz—I'm a pilot, Henry. So I watch clearances."

Mr. Reiter chalked my bravado up to "New York moxie."

I explained, "It helps that I don't own the car."

My driving skills were playing better and better.

Some forty minutes later, as I was driving Miss Coplan from the Waldorf-Astoria to the hotel, trying to pass a white Lincoln Continental on my right, Miss Coplan confessed, "I could never drive in New York."

"It would make you too anxious?" I asked.

"Ye—"

Boom!

Just as Miss Coplan started to respond in the affirmative, I accidentally sideswiped the Lincoln in a textbook case of Bad Clearance. I slammed on the brakes. So *this* was the uh-oh feeling.

"Is there damage?" Miss Coplan asked.

My heart started hammering. A Long-Islandy woman in her fifties got out of the driver's seat of the car. I could see only a small scrape.

"My husband is disabled. Hold on."

Her husband, wearing pastel clothing and white shoes, got out of the car and waddled over. He surveyed the Lincoln for damage, hunching over as much as he could to inspect its chromestripping. Then, finally, he waved his hand to dismiss us.

I did not look Miss Coplan in the eyes for eighteen hours after this incident. When, back at the hotel, she made a series of calls from the pay phone, I became convinced that my services would shortly be terminated. But she never mentioned the incident.

That being the opening night of the convention, I knew we would have to be vigilant in our attempt to get close to the Garden. Avenues had been shut down, barricades had been erected; the size of the crowd of policemen outside the hotel suggested the unexpected discovery of a vault full of doughnuts. At about four-thirty, as we approached a police-man who was blocking cars from entering Thirty-fourth Street at Ninth Avenue—a location some two blocks from the Garden—I lowered my voice and said as authoritatively as possible to him, "I have the governor of Colorado, Sir." This failed to produce the desired effect; he motioned us south. We proceeded in that direction, and some six min-utes later we found ourselves circling back. When we got to another barricade at Thirty-fourth Street and Tenth Ave-nue, the governor, who at the time was being interviewed by a CNN reporter over his cellular phone, told the reporter to wait a minute; then he lowered his window and barked, "I'm Roy Romer from Colorado. I'm on the Democratic Platform Committee. How do I get into the Garden?" The policeman—perhaps out of some heretofore-inexpressible allegiance to the Platform Committee—removed the barri-cade and we zoomed down Thirty-fourth Street. However, there still remained the matter of the policeman who had rebuffed us earlier at Thirty-fourth and Ninth. Surely the fact that the other officer had let us through would give us some leverage in our negotiations; but would it be enough?

As I drove into the intersection, planning to sidle up to the officer and plead our case, Mr. Reiter said to me, "Floor it. Just go right past him." I did, experiencing a surge of adrenaline; because I was cringing, I did not see the policeman's reaction.

TUESDAY

On Tuesday morning I asked the garage attendant if I could park the car near the garage exit for ten or fifteen minutes. I explained that I was picking up Governor Romer of Colorado. He agreed; when he had brought the car up from the basement, I gave him a five-dollar bill. Tip or bribe: I was not sure.

When Miss Coplan came out, I explained that I had been parking quite a lot at the hotel but that I had not been asked for any cash; the attendants were simply taking down the number on our parking cards and then keeping track of our hours in the ledger.

She said, "Well if they say anything . . ."

"Just say 'Ron Brown, Suite 4510?' "

"Right."

At about eight-thirty A.M. I parked the car fifty feet from the entrance to the Hotel Beverly, where the governor was meeting with the Colorado delegates. An angry female DOT worker, dressed in a reflective red vest and a brown cap, knocked on my partially open window and yelled, "Move up to the middle! This is a loading zone!"

"I'm picking up the governor," I told her.

"You'll have to move up!"

"I have to be here in case he comes out."

"This is not a parking space!"

She was yelling very close to my ear.

"The guy I'm picking up is the governor of Colorado *and* of Arizona."

"I don't care if he's the president of the United States, move up!"

I moved the car about eight inches forward; she crossed the street and left me alone. When the governor and Miss Thornberry emerged shortly thereafter, they praised my parking spot and told me I was doing a good job.

At noon we were unable to get the car out of the Hilton garage; the impending departure of Bill Clinton from the hotel via a rear exit had thrown the carport into a frenzy of security measures and press people. Mr. Reiter and the governor, like flies to raw meat, positioned themselves right in the exitway just across from the camera crews and photographers. Hillary Clinton came out first and talked to Governor Romer for about a minute; then Clinton joined them for about as long. The blinding effulgence of TV lights as they bounced off reflective surfaces was like being too close to welding.

When Mr. Reiter and the governor were finally able to get into our car some six minutes later, Mr. Reiter had the kind of smile that I associate with men who have just reeled in very large fish. "They were talkin' ag. policy!" he said with some elation.

In the late afternoon I saw Ted Kennedy walk through the lobby of the Hilton; I was glad to have my own bad driving put into a historical context.

As Miss Coplan had secured me credentials to get into the convention each night—a true act of generosity, particularly given that most drivers did not get in—I was able to see Governor Romer, in his capacity as cochairman of the Platform Committee, address the convention that evening; I felt like a proud parent.

WEDNESDAY

While we drove back to the hotel after a six-thirty A.M. live interview on CNN, a cab suddenly pulled in front of us at Forty-sixth Street and Eighth Avenue. I slammed on the brakes.

"Jesus!" the governor gasped.

But the day's more knotty transportation problem was how to get the governor to a softball game in Central Park when most of the roads to the park were closed. Pitting the Coloradan delegates against the Hawaiian delegates, the game was being held on the field near the Carousel. I called four different people for directions, including the woman who organized the game and the man from the Parks Department who issued the permit for the game; I got four different answers. I ended up parking at Seventh Avenue and Fifty-ninth Street and telling the governor and his staff to walk 350 yards north.

When they emerged from the park some fifty minutes later, the governor, having removed his tie and suit jacket and put on a pair of black sneakers, was sweating profusely, his loose shirttails flapping with each step he took. Mr. Reiter explained to me that the governor had caught a line drive.

"He caught it just like this," he said, miming the governor's catch. "TV got the whole thing. You couldn't have *scripted* it better."

They got in the car, the backseat sending forth a waft of vinegary Romer-roma.

As we drove to the Beekman Tower, the governor spoke via cellular phone to a prison official in Denver. In the middle of the conversation, he asked Mr. Reiter for a pad of paper. What then happened left a permanent scar on my memory: Mr. Reiter, reaching for the clipboard that I carried each day, removed my copy of the governor's daily schedule from it, and *handed the governor the pad on which I had been keeping notes for this story.*

It is with some hesitation that I try to describe the ensuing two minutes, so inextricably linked in my mind are they with the phrase *weltering abdominal cramps*. I racked my brains trying to remember if I had torn off the last completed page of notes and put it in my jacket pocket, as I had been trying to do regularly; I could not remember. The specter of incarceration swept across my consciousness like cloud patterns on a weather map. My bowels went soft.

Finally, the governor concluded his phone call, ripped off

the page he was writing on and returned the pad, saying nothing.

THURSDAY

On the morning of the final day of the convention, the governor's staff spent much time phoning people who might have influence over the evening's telecast. Their mission was to see that Governor Romer would be standing on the platform as part of Bill Clinton's backdrop. Miss Thornberry told someone at the Democratic Governors' Association that she had watched part of the convention on TV the night before, saying, "I think the picture that we had last night—of Tom Foley and all those Congressional people—is not the picture we want tonight. I really feel that Bill's backdrop should be the governors of this country." To a second person she suggested not that the governors of this country be on the platform, but that the cochairs of the Platform Committee of this country be. Meanwhile, the governor expressed concern that he was not "connected enough" with the Clinton campaign, saying, "If I could go over there and walk through the campaign headquarters just so they know I'm alive."

Indeed, I, too, was still having problems impressing the parking attendants and DOT workers of New York by dropping the governor's name. While I was waiting for the governor and his staff outside the Doral Tuscany, a large male DOT worker came over to the car and said that, although he didn't mind my parking in the hotel loading zone, he felt I was "inconveniencing" the truck behind me. I moved all of six feet, to the other end of the loading zone; the man returned.

"I'm waiting for the governor of Colorado and Barbra Streisand," I said.

"She's here, too?" he asked without interest.

"Yeah. She's a delegate from Guam."

"Well, you're gonna have to move."

"My problem is that Barbra is in a leotard. I don't want her to have to—"

"You need to move, sir."

I moved.

While I later drove Miss Coplan from the credentials office to the InterContinental, she called Miss Thornberry and explained to her that the people at the Democratic Governors' Association "had spoken to Ickes"—I assumed this meant convention manager Harold Ickes—and he had agreed to bring the governors up on stage after the acceptance speech. Upon disengaging the cellular phone, Miss Coplan said, "That was too easy. This can't be right."

When I had dropped the governor and staff off at the Garden, the discussion turned to whether I should run out and get the car ready during Clinton's acceptance speech, or whether I should hear the whole speech, and then run out and get the car ready.

"Listen to the acceptance speech and then come on

out," Miss Thornberry said. "You should listen to it. After all this bullshit, you deserve it."

Because Mr. Reiter had left the entourage earlier that day, I was given his credentials and was thus granted access to that vaunted location within the convention, the floor. I savored the irony that I, a driver, had gotten a floor pass when many of my journalist friends had been denied one. My interest in the proceedings of the convention trebled. What had previously seemed a fairly stock series of speeches was now, at times, truly rousing. I felt very close to "the process."

When it came time to drive the group back to the hotel, I was feeling emboldened. Flush with the dynamism of democratic ideals, I started to race the lights up Sixth Avenue. For the first time in six days, I used the car horn to admonish other drivers.

"Oh my God," Miss Thornberry said. "He's completely transformed into a cabbie."

After I had dropped the group off and bid them goodbye, I pulled into the garage. The attendant gazed at me wearily.

"Ron Brown," I said. "Suite 4510."

LIFESTYLING

How to Do Everything

As I trudge, burrolike, ever deeper into the valley of advanced age, I am increasingly struck by the realization that I have stopped developing new interests and skills. Life, it often appears, is more and more a reassertion of old and somewhat tired themes; new topics of potential inquiry are lost amidst a regimen of seeing current movies, patronizing ethnic restaurants, and making uncharitable comments about those not immediately present.

Thus, when I apprised myself of the opportunities offered by the ever-burgeoning instructional video market, I pledged to inject my torpor with the shock of the new. Indeed, be it a language, a sport, or a technique for turning travel brochures into "one-of-a-kind wearables and accessories," a huge number of endeavors can now be pursued by videotape—the aspiring ambassador of human relations can learn How to Deal with Difficult People; the aspiring angler can learn how to "locate schools of crappies and imitate their food sources."

I hastened to the Upper East Side location of New York City's How To Video Source. As I browsed through the store's more than twelve hundred titles, I fixated on the frightening illustration on the jacket of *The Art of Hair Transplantation* and the length of rope included with *Trick and Fancy Roping;* however, I put both tapes back, loath as I am to involve myself with either tweezers or chaps. But overall, I found that my selections were braver than they would have been had I been applying for a class; chief among the pleasures of video learning is the realization that you will never be forced to wear a leotard in the presence of total strangers.

In my first foray into the world of instructional videos, I chose a tape called *Blooming Visions for Beginners.* Hosted by a smiley, middle-aged woman named Carol Smith, this tape teaches you how to use Blooming Visions liquid bisque (sold separately) in order to make "beautiful, bisquelike sculpture" that does not require firing. Much of the tape consists of close-ups of Carol's glamor-length nails wrangling arts and crafts supplies that have been drenched in what looks like pudding. From the three projects demonstrated on the tape, I chose Carol's personal favorite: "Project #3, the Spilled Daisy Pot."

Per Carol's instructions, I dipped actual daisies and Spanish moss into liquid bisque, and arranged them so that they appeared to have tumbled out of a tipped-over flowerpot.

My hands thoroughly goopy, I used my elbow to turn my VCR off while I waited for my sculpture to dry. When I returned to the tape, Carol, her glamor-lengths now debisqued, showed me how to paint the flowers and moss, deftly "feathering" with a small brush, "hazing" with a large brush, and "spattering" with a toothbrush. Then she encouraged me to paint the terra-cotta pot itself with Persimmon, a color she describes as "luscious."

My resultant Spilled Daisy Pot is lovely—the arts and crafts equivalent of Jell-O salad with miniature marshmallows. Given that the desired look is that of something that has been "laying out in the garden for a while," I feel that my piece is particularly successful. Carol warns the viewer never to coat cookies, vegetables, or bread with liquid bisque; I have bravely curbed this temptation.

Of the many tapes that I watched, the one that proved most difficult was the exhilarating *Curso de Rumba de la Luz*—authentic Latin instruction on how to dance the rumba. Emphasizing every third beat in its 4/4 time signature, this Cuban dance requires its participants do three things at once: rattle off highly rhythmic, tap-dance-like footwork; flourish and twirl your hands in a roiling, undulant manner; and keep your carriage erect and impervious to bounce. While you do these, your demeanor should be simultaneously tragic and urgent, as if you have been shot in the stomach and are late for an appointment. Taking my cues from the tape's *bien apasionado* male dancer, Adrian "El Chino" (Adrian "the Chinese"), I could not help but feel intensely Caucasian; I soon realized that I was at a distinct disadvantage in owning no clothing that has been shrink-wrapped to my pelvis.

Nevertheless, after honing my rumba technique for some four hours over the course of a week, I told my friend Carrie that I would make her dinner one night and then take her out to rumba. When she arrived at my apartment, her eyes widened with amazement: I had, through an application of the skills demonstrated on yet another tape, *How to Garnish,* transformed my kitchen into a winter wonderland of colorful vegetable garnishes. My kitchen table was host to ten tropically colored, canteloupe-sized Onion Mums (you slice the onions longitudinally, soak them in hot water to remove their odor, and then dip them in food coloring); in close proximity was my South Seas Island Scene featuring a Cucumber Shark and palm trees rendered with green pepper fronds atop notched carrot trunks. And, basking midway between land and sea, was my adorable Lemon Pig. "You have too much time on your hands!" Carrie gasped when she had taken it all in. Indeed, my labors may have been overkill for a casual dinner *a deux;* in my anxiety about exposing my rumba skills to the harsh light of the outside world, I may have overgarnished.

After we had supped on a delicious veal stew, I explained to Carrie that I had included in the stew's ingredients the corks from three bottles of wine. I had been initiated into this practice—it tenderizes the meat through the release of the corks' enzymes—by *Trucs of the Trade,* a tape in which various chefs proffer culinary tips and secrets, *truc* being

French for *gimmick*. Given, I suppose, that the veal was quite tender, the revelation of the wine cork *truc* did not cause Carrie to blanch; more alarming to her, it seemed, was my subsequent *truc*, wherein I pulled a crème brûlée out of my refrigerator and proceeded to brown it with a blowtorch. As Hubert Keller, the chef of San Francisco's Fleur de Lys, explains in his heavy accent on the tape, "You see it turns very, very quickly a nice golden brown color."

Located seven blocks from my apartment is New York City's premier showcase of live Latin music, S.O.B.'s (Sounds of Brazil). Thus, when Carrie and I had blithely trundled off to S.O.B.'s, it was with a note of confusion that we read, just outside the club's portals, a sign encouraging passersby to thrill to the music of a band called Raïna Raï that had come "Direct from Algeria." Our perplexity about the non-Latin nature of this offering was matched only by our bewilderment that Algeria acknowledges the umlaut. Nevertheless, we entered; I proceeded to emulate the fiery choreographic bravura of Adrian "El Chino." That I did some of my best footwork and fingerwork ever was no doubt due to my realization that, if there were ever going to be a situation in which I would feel comfortable doing the rumba, it would be deep inside a throng of gyrating Algerians.

Jugglercise came more naturally to me. This eponymous tape, which comes with three eighteen-inch-square fluorescent scarves, is hosted by an irksome man in a mortarboard and gown named Professor Confidence. We learn how to juggle the scarves (an activity more strenuous than you might imagine); the rest of the tape features folky music videos by which to juggle. Standing in front of my television, grabbing and clawing in vain at the air, I was not sure at first whether to keep my eyes on the tape or the scarves; I was reminded of the climactic scenes of *The Sorcerer's Apprentice*. However, within several hours I was able to muster a fairly steady volley of fluorescence—a sort of Dance of the Seven Veils shot through with the fragrance of peanuts and sawdust. I then moved on to the Column (scarves are thrown straight up) and the Reverse Cascade (scarves are thrown counterclockwise instead of clockwise). Indeed, I even devised my own trademark throw in which scarves originating near my stomach are thrown out in front of me; I call this throw Scarves Are Coming Out of My Body.

=

The strangest tape that I encountered was *Sybervision Bowling*. This tape, a neuromuscular approach to bowling, contains no talking or instructions, only a sonorous, *Chariots of Fire*–like music track laid over hundreds of repeated sequences, many in slow motion, of two professional bowlers continually knocking all ten pins down. According to the tape's workbook, as the viewer immerses himself in the "beautiful images of movement performed by a model athlete," his nervous system is "excited" and "reacts as if it were physically performing the skill"; this neural excitement is translated into "neuromuscular memory."

I followed the tape's 30-Day Training Program, watching part of the tape each day and then trying to reimagine it in the "imaginary screen" of my mind. (The workbook also mentions locating the "imaginary screen" in your abdomen, but I found this, like the segment in *How to Garnish* in which a carrot is thrust deep inside a hollowed-out cucumber, too upsetting to pursue.) Rewinding the tape to the section that I wanted each day was not always easy; this is not a tape whose individual scenes are startlingly unique. That the slow motion segments of the video are meant to "promote within you a feeling of confidence—'He makes it look so simple and smooth. It is simple! I can do that!'— and a desire to bowl" did not quite resonate with me; it was also difficult, when bowling, to imagine myself a "great bowler [I] admire," given that my most vivid memories of bowlers are of the other third graders at Benjie Garfield's eighth birthday party. I did, however, become all a-tingle whenever I watched the two-and-a-half-minute-long climax of the "Striking" segment of the tape, consisting of ninety rapid close-ups of the ball smashing into the pins, each close-up complete with the "sweetpot sound" of the struck pins; one day I watched this sequence fourteen times in a row and then *rushed* to the lanes (scores: 72, 110). In the end, my game improved but continued to be erratic.

Another tape that required repeated viewing was *Berlitz's German for Travelers*. After you watch two actors who play characters named Mr. and Mrs. Bell speak German in various actual settings (a bank, a café, etc.), you are then shown each scene again, only this time *you* provide both of the Bells' dialogue. Talking to my television as both man and

woman was quite fun, appealing as it did to my ever-present
desire to be a German transvestite; I searched my apartment
in vain for photographer Helmut Newton.

One afternoon, having practiced for several days all of the
scenes that involved eating or buying, I nervously headed
off to Yorkville, the German area of Manhattan's Upper
East Side, and found a bakery. After canvasing the bakery's
offerings, I asked the dour, elderly woman behind the display case, "Voss *kone*-en zee *oonz* empf-fallen?" ("What can
you recommend?"), whereupon she rattled off an in-
timidating series of sounds wholly unintelligible to me. She
then pointed at a confection rich with frosting and cherries;
I countered with a phrase from the "Shopping" section of
the tape wherein the odious Mrs. Bell, looking for a blouse
at a clothing store, had terrorized the sales help—"Nine,
das ist *nicked* gahnz mine guh-*schmocked*" ("No, that is not
my taste"). The woman gave me a sour look, as if I had
personally insulted her grandchildren. *"Bit*-tuh," I added
hurriedly, fearful that she was going to alert the manager to
my presence, "Ick *murk*-tuh ein *shtook* hazelnut torte"
("Please, I'd like a slice Hazelnut Torte"). When she then
asked me a series of incomprehensible and increasingly urgent questions, my mind suddenly filled with the graphics
from a tape I had watched earlier that day, *Witness Prepara-
tion for Giving Depositions*—"Tell the Truth!" "Listen to
the Entire Question!" "Don't Volunteer Information!"
Finally, when it became clear that she was asking if I wanted
to sit at a table, I pointed at the street and improvised,

"Nine *donk*-uh, *stross*-uh ist fear goot" ("No thank you, street is very good").

That evening, still slightly rattled, I watched the first two tapes of *Stress Management for Professionals*. After having had to rumba, jugglercise, imagine bowling, and speak German to the more interactive videos, watching this taped lecture about stress was like taking a long, hot bath. Most notable about this commonsensical series hosted by therapist Roger Mellott is the number of metaphors, mostly food-related, that he manages to fit into three hours of lecturing. People are full of "tea" (egocentrism). Like monkeys, we hold on to "bananas" (issues that we exaggerate the importance of). We are prey to the "artichoke theory" (spending too much time on the outside leaves instead of the core). We need to learn to "spend our pie" (expend our energy) more effectively by "slicing our salami" (dealing with problems one at a time). If we don't, we'll get "pizza burns" (signs of stress).

What should we do? Mr. Mellott, in addition to extolling the virtues of writing, exercising, and crying, suggests that we occasionally let go of the "marbles" (problems and stress) that we have "swallowed" by talking them through in a six-minute "verbal marble dump." He suggests that we dump on a household pet. Because I do not have a pet, I used my aloe plant. Pressing the pause button, I sat on the couch in front of my television and unloaded the burdens of my psyche on my unsuspecting plant. I was reminded of *How to Be a Ventriloquist*, wherein our host talks about how shy and introverted children often repress thoughts and feelings. "Believe me," he says, referring to his dummy, Knucklehead Smiff, "having a little partner that I could control gave me the opportunity to say many of those things and took off quite a bit of pressure." When I had put my own "little partner" back on the kitchen windowsill, I realized that, yes, I was feeling relieved; but I couldn't help but feel that there must be some more expedient means to the same end. Sex? Therapy? Keening? And then it hit me: I switched off the VCR. Then I took a crème brûlée from the refrigerator and strafed it with my blowtorch.

WHAT IF YOUR MOVING MEN WERE MERCHANT AND IVORY?

11:00 A.M.   **Helena Bonham Carter arrives bearing drop cloth and addled spinster.**

11:45 A.M.   **Daniel Day-Lewis puts on spats, refers to fire escape as *loggia*.**

12:13 A.M.   **Maggie Smith announces that loose items on truck can cause "quite a kerfuffle."**

1:19 P.M.   **Julian Sands arrives with scratch remover and local vicar.**

3:25 P.M.   **Emma Thompson puts down packing crate; has epiphany on sofa.**

4:04 P.M.   **Phone call: Ruth Prawer Jhabvala has been lost in baggage claim of foreign airport.**

5:25 P.M.   **Filmmakers arrive; they reminisce, fondle wicker.**

WHAT IF MACY'S WERE TURNED INTO
A CORRECTIONAL CENTER?

10:03 A.M.   Inmates play poker in Moderate Shoes, using mannequin heads to ante.

10:55 A.M.   Lifer enters Bridal Registry; updates list.

12:21 P.M.   Inmate tells social worker of desire to sodomize regional buyer.

2:40 P.M.   Inmate announces to guard, "The lesbian has stolen my cigarettes."

3:38 P.M.   Inmate emerges from underneath basement bargain bin carrying dirt from tunnel; surreptitiously dumps dirt on Le Petit Cafe's display of international coffees.

4:10 P.M.   Group of inmates convene to hear noted gardening author C. Z. Guest discuss peat.

6:00 P.M.   Inmates file into basement deli for dinner; inmate bangs crystal goblet against Calphalon in overture to riot.

WHAT IF BALLET DANCERS WERE
SUBJECT TO LEASH LAWS?

9:13 A.M. Tension from dancer's collar and leash unsnaps Danskin crotch panel.

9:23 A.M. Dancer is momentarily asphyxiated during a series of pirouettes.

12:20 P.M. Dancer tied to tree outside restaurant rubs chafed neck, applies lotion.

2:46 P.M. Tourist mistakes stray dachshund for a haggard Gelsey Kirkland.

3:30 P.M. Bitter choreographer illustrates command "Heel!" by swatting at dancer's ankles with heavy cane.

Circus Jerks

Although the idea of being a circus clown has held appeal for me ever since childhood, the practicalities of learning the trade have always kept me at bay: I would not enjoy getting into a tiny car and sitting very, very close to other members of my profession; I do not want to litter my friends' homes with my failed balloon art; I am not anxious to have seltzer down my pants. However, when a magazine editor told me that a singles resort in Negril, Jamaica, was, in an attempt to lure guests during the off-peak season, holding a circus workshop in which it would bring "all the excitement of the big tent to its sandy white beach on the Caribbean Sea," the inherent graciousness of resort living allowed me to abandon my preconceptions and accept the assignment. I called the resort's publicist and said, "*Les junkets—je les adore.*"

=

Two days before I was to leave, I called the singles-oriented resort and asked if there was any special circus-related clothing or equipment that I needed to bring; the woman who answered the phone said she could think of nothing.

"If I bring a broom," I asked her, "could I be the little clown who sweeps up the spotlight at the end of the circus?"

Her training had apparently not prepared her for this question. I was put on hold; seconds later the line disconnected.

I packed a broom.

Upon my arrival at the lovely, palm-dappled grounds, a young Jamaican man, one of the resort's employees, carried my bag into my room and assured me in a lilting patois, "You are going to have the ball of your life." I told him I was quite excited about the circus workshop; he smiled indulgently and said that if I maintained proximity to him throughout my stay, I would be introduced to the most beautiful of the female guests and would "definitely score." I thanked him for his vote of confidence. My room contained two mirrors—one, about five by two feet, was directly in front of the bed; the other, about five by five feet, was directly over the bed.

On the sunshiny, palm-lined beach I found a trampoline, a trapeze, and a high wire—all in excellent condition, none in use. I searched for other evidence of the circus arts but found only sunbathing and lapsed *Nacktkultur*. At dinner I thought I'd discovered an aerialist in the tubby, slightly balding man who was walking around the dining room wearing nothing but a black G-string; but someone explained to me that he was "in computers" and from Chicago. When my eyes chanced upon a woman in the dinner line wearing suspenders, I thought that I had at last found a fellow clown. But when I walked over to her I discovered that her suspenders were buoying not baggy pants but bare breasts—the better to display the shimmery gold chain that linked her two pierced nipples.

As I struck up conversations with various of the 250 or so guests during my stay, it became increasingly clear that few of them had come for the circus workshop. As it turned out, this was fortunate for them: the circus sessions for the next two days were canceled because of rain. I contemplated calling the resort's publicist back in New York but decided simply to allow events to unfold on their own.

During the rainy afternoons, the resort's employees organized group games in the dining room. In one game, volunteers from the audience were paired off with members of the opposite sex and were then encouraged to ask each other provocative questions. Thus, just as I was taking my fourth bite of delicious fresh pineapple one day, the p.a. system broadcast a giggly woman saying to a man seated across from her, "Hi. I'm Ellen from Florida. Have you ever done it in Crisco or in oil?" whereupon the man responded, "Hi. I'm Bruce from Washington. Yes, with baby oil once." Other facts that the guests deemed important to broadcast over loudspeakers included, "Do you strap on when using a big dildo?" "Have you ever been fist-fucked?" and "Have you ever licked a man's asshole?" Another game was a version of Loser's Bingo wherein players tried to be the last person standing. The categories started on a fairly tame level ("Sit down if your birthday is in July") but then, when the group was reduced to six women, became increasingly unsavory ("Sit down if you swallow"). When a forties-ish, raw-boned woman responded to the command "Sit down if you gave a blow job last night," she was accorded a smattering of applause.

=

I did not participate in these games. I was not sure how to react. I thought about my predecessors; I wondered what the immortal Emmett Kelly and Slivers Oakley would have done in my place. How would Otto Griebling, the most beloved joey to ever tramp the sawdust, have handled this situation? I did not know. All I knew was that I have certain professional limits. Which is to say, *I don't work blue.*

=

In the course of my ruminations, the dining room had given way to a toga-tying demonstration for that evening's toga party. We were reminded repeatedly that if we didn't wear a toga to dinner, we wouldn't be served ("No sheet, no eat") and that if we wore underwear under our togas, our underwear would be cut off.

I began to feel slightly anxious. A maid brought a bed

sheet to my room. As I nervously wrapped my pale body, it gradually became clear that the finer points of the toga-tying demonstration had eluded me; the toga I fashioned was melancholic and larval. I skulked into the dining room and beheld a multiplicity of elaborate toga fashions. Guests had brought accessories and props from home—one man had used a fern, sunglasses, and a necktie to anthropomorphize a three-foot-long bulbous trunk that dangled from his crotch.

Dinner gave way to the Guest Talent Show—perhaps at last the demonstration of the clowning abilities I craved. Alas, I was disappointed again. One act, the Candy Lickers, consisted of two highly Nautilized men with all-over tans wearing only G-strings and matching cowboy boots. They sashayed onto the floor to music whose lyrics were a combination of filth and bad rhyming. They coaxed three blonde volunteers out of the audience and seated them, one at a time, on a stool, then craned their heads toward each woman's crotch and commenced licking the air. By the end of her stay onstage, each of the women had mustered a tight smile or forced laughter, but even a novice clown such as myself knew that they were crying on the inside.

Later that night, after the excitement of the talent show had subsided, many guests reconvened in the dining room for the regular evening snack hour. A man placed a chair on the stage where the Lickers had done their work and proceeded to watch, mesmerized, as his female companion removed her top and danced erotically to music being played on the stereo system. He drew the woman close to him and nuzzled and fondled her breasts. About twelve guests gradually drifted away from the snack table and toward this display. Among them was the other night's publicly confessed blow-job woman, who, sitting alone, looked on while rhapsodically snacking on a tiny cheese sandwich.

A bibulous woman in her late twenties introduced herself to me and asked me my name. I told her it was Sweepy; she asked me to spell it. I did, and then she asked me whether the name was Dutch. I explained that I was a clown and that Sweepy was my stage name; she held her ground by telling me I looked Dutch.

On my next-to-last day, the weather finally permitted a trapeze workshop to be held. A mere five guests materialized. Our instructor was charming and informative: Within a couple of hours I was able, while swinging back and forth some twenty feet above the ground, to hang from the bar by my knees. I thanked the instructor and quickly retreated to my room.

Later I soaked in a jacuzzi, played squash by myself, and walked on the dizzyingly beautiful moonlit beach. I did not opt to rejoin the other guests, who continued to swing in nontrapeze fashion. As I reflected on the previous three days, it occurred to me that, with respect to this particular writing assignment, the joke had most assuredly been on me.

I longed to return to the city, to escape the predicament of having gotten a proverbial pie in the face.

WHAT IF MAYOR MCCHEESE WROTE
A TELL-ALL AUTOBIOGRAPHY?

WHAT IF YOUR CATS OPENED
A HELLENIC DINER?

2:13 P.M.   Waitress-cat gives you placemat emblazoned with the history of feta.

2:14 P.M.   Proprietor-cat places bust of *Born Free*'s Elsa on Ionic column fragment.

2:24 P.M.   Waitress-cat explains that kitchen is out of the Bagel Fantasy and the scrod.

2:30 P.M.   Dishwasher-cat enters statuary nook for licking and scratching.

3:10 P.M.   Elderly waiter-cat leaves counter duty to nap at register.

WHAT IF SANTA'S WORKSHOP PRODUCED PERFORMANCE ART IN THE OFF-SEASON?

February Elf performs show utilizing African narrative, laser art, deaf signing, and piles of garbage.

March Elf arrives late to all rehearsals in attempt to create aura.

April Santa performs nine-hour show in Tibetan mime and Urdu.

May Santa calls Ottawa to place large order of yams.

June Elf uses leftover ribbon to strap Vocoder onto Blitzen.

July Rudolph offers monodrama, *Reindeer Games I Never Played: A Show About Healing.*

August Mrs. Claus walks onstage wearing beauty pageant banners and raw beef slabs.

September Elf's same five friends see his show for the forty-seventh time.

Someone's in the Kitchen

Julia Child, Shirley MacLaine, and Gerald Ford have all done it at the Park Avenue Café. The Associated Press and the Culinary Institute of America have done it at the Waldorf-Astoria. Tama Janowitz and Matt Dillon have done it at the Plaza Hotel; when they were finished, each graced the guestbook with comments rendered in an inimitable prose style (Miss Janowitz: "What a fantastic experience. As if birds, rubies, moths, and other entities descended from the sky and became food in one's mouth." Mr. Dillon: "Excellent grub.")

Enter, if you will, the stately and elegant Edwardian Room of the Plaza Hotel. Behold the high, majestic oak-and-mahogany-paneled ceiling, the walls drenched in scarlet damask, the views of horse-drawn carriages ready for hire; savor the tantalizing aroma of delicacies wafting tableward. The lovely petit-point armchair in front of you? Do not sit on it. No, come this way, please, into the kitchen—as Miss Janowitz and Mr. Dillon did, as Sting and David Lynch have, as David Hockney, John McEnroe, Dean Stockwell, Louise Bourgeois, Julian Schnabel, and the members of INXS have—past the gray and moldering mop, past the dozing busboy. It is here, amidst the heat and bustle—a step or two from the fragrant dishwashing station, hard by the plastic bin harboring soiled towels—that you will find what you are looking for: your dinner table.

=

"Is it . . . private?" I asked the Plaza employee who was taking my reservation.

"We'll just set a table for two," he told me.

"Right," I said. "But I mean, will we be able to have a private conversation? My wife has a tendency to, to sob in restaurants."

"The kitchen is a very busy place."

"But we'll be able to hear ourselves talk," I said.

"Oh, yes," he responded.

"Okay," I said. "We'll see you next Thursday."

=

It was in the dizzy 1980s, when so many people had so much money that there just weren't enough choice tables in the dining room to accommodate them all, that the Plaza solved the problem of making the important guest feel his importantness among legions of merely significant diners: Let him eat in the kitchen. Now, with evidence clear that the very people who faint at the prospect of being seated *near* the kitchen leap at the chance to dine *in* it, restaurants throughout New York City are inviting VIP customers to break bread where others are baking it.

When asked about the inclination to eat in the sweltry and clamorous kitchen of a restaurant—an inclination that can be indulged on a prix-fixed basis at the aforementioned places, as well as at Tatou and the French Culinary Institute in New York, Charlie Trotter's in Chicago, and the Raleigh Hotel in Miami—Margaret Visser, the author of *The Rituals of Dinner* and *Much Depends on Dinner,* pointed out, "In the early days of the theater, the nobility sat on the stage." Indeed; and in the case of eating grillside, sometimes the nobility *perform* on the stage: When dining in the kitchen of Arcadia (now discontinued), Burgess Meredith used to compose sonnets and sing songs of homage to the Beaujolais; when given a negligee at her birthday party in the kitchen of the Edwardian Room one year, rocker Debbie Harry shucked her clothes in a closet near the waiters' podium and, in making her way back to the kitchen, scampered through the dining room in the negligee and high heels.

In other instances, diners experience not a feeling of expansion and liberation, but rather one of entrapment. At the Park Avenue Café, David Burke's sublime, inventive food is served to diners who sit in an air-conditioned, soundproof box, two sides of which are glass. Waiters peer in from the sides to note your progress; they deposit mounds of food and then depart, quickly sliding the door shut—it's like day care, but catered. "You're in *the middle of the kitchen*," emphasized Clark Wolf, the restaurant consultant, about dining in the kitchen of the Edwardian Room. "This one woman we were with was wearing a low-cut dress. She dropped a little bit of sauce someplace . . . *critical*," said Wolf. "And just watched it melt."

=

"Do you think it's a little . . . weird for us to be here?" I asked our charming busboy, Balegh, midway through our meal in the Plaza's kitchen.

"Well, no," he said. "Many people find it very nice, very interesting."

"But aren't we in the way?" I asked.

"Not so much. We don't do it on the busiest nights."

"Because then we would get trampled on," I surmised.

"Yes, this could happen then."

=

Peoples' motives for enduring this particular form of hardship vary. For the food-obsessive, of course, eating in the kitchen is the ultimate insider activity, an opportunity to buy admission to the exclusivity of the ages-old chef's table, that phenomenon wherein a chef and his staff achieve commensality (meaning, literally, "togetherness arising out of the fact that we eat at the same table") by eating together in the kitchen before the dinner rush. Some partake in order to effect quality control: "I've never been served a bad dish in a restaurant's kitchen," said *Gourmet*'s New York restaurant reviewer, Andy Birsh. Some partake in order to give voice to the health inspector who lurks within: "You can see how clean the kitchen is," noted Michel Richard, the proprietor of Hollywood's Citrus.

Restaurants have other ways, of course, of accommodating Americans' fascination with the process of cooking and their need to make a celebrity of the person grilling their infant zucchini. Large pieces of plate glass at places like Citrus, Smith and Wollensky, the Tasting Room at Le Bernadin, and Brendan Walsh's North Street Grill in Great Neck, New York, afford the diners views of the chef in his domain (indeed, Citrus diners recently broke into applause at the sight of the bearded, pear-shaped Michel Richard dancing the French cancan on a kitchen counter with a customer); a sushi-bar-like "food bar" at Zoë in New York City allows diners to talk to the chef ("I don't want it," said one customer to chef Steven Levine when he saw Levine garnishing an entrée, "Your hands were on it"). Sometimes video is used to bridge the gap between dining room and kitchen—a nineteen-inch color video monitor located at the bar of City restaurant in Los Angeles captures all the splendor and excitement of the kitchen's grill area and tandoori oven; video cameras hidden in the dining room of Pierre Orsi in Lyons, France, allow the chef to gauge diners' reactions to his offerings.

But, as compared with these more dispassionate, clinical interchanges, eating in the kitchen stems more from a desire for intimacy. "It's a very ambivalent thing," said Margaret Visser. "On the one hand, diners are creating a tremendous distance between themselves and the cooks, they're being very judgmental and are expecting extreme competence and lots of entertainment; and on the other hand, they want to feel all homey."

And, of course, they want highly exciting, labor-intensive food—food that is somehow different and better than that available to the hoi polloi in the dining room. It is on this count that meals eaten in the kitchen rarely fail to deliver. During chef Kerry Simon's reign at the Edwardian Room, waiters made great ceremony of the untying of the cord that bound Simon's black squid ink lasagna in its sheath of green banana leaves; a recent meal at that same location concluded with, among other elaborate confections, delicious fresh poached apricots and apricot sorbet afloat on something called an "almond doughnut abstract."

=

"Did you say, 'almond doughnut abstract'?" I asked the dessert chef.

"Yes."

"That sounds . . . exciting," I said.

"Where did you get fresh apricots?" Erica, my dinner-mate, asked.

"We're a hotel."

"And are there other kinds of doughnut abstract?" I asked.

"You can do others," he said. "But for now it's just the almond."

=

But all standards of excessiveness pale in comparison to those of the by-invitation-only Annual Game Dinner, held in the 12,400-square-foot kitchen of the Perona Farms banquet facility in Andover, New Jersey. Attended by two hundred people in 1993, including chefs Pierre Franey, Daniel Boulud, Jean-Louis Palladin (Jean-Louis of the Watergate Hotel, Washington), Jean-François Taquet (Taquet's, Philadelphia), Gordon Drysdale (Bix, San Francisco), Francesco Ricchi (I Ricchi, Washington) and then *New York Times* restaurant reviewer Bryan Miller, the twelfth annual feast (and benefit for the National Multiple Sclerosis Society) consisted of fifty-two courses. Much of the food is hunted and fished by the guests, many of whom wear their hunting clothes; "stag" videos of the hunting and fishing expeditions that produced the food are shown throughout the meal on two TV monitors.

A variety of unusual foodstuffs has been offered over the years, including elk tacos and goose breast jerky. 1993's menu featured a veritable chorus line of the poultry world (Goose Legs Rillette, Woodcock Legs Tempura, Wild Duck Legs Salmi with Burgundy Wine, Stuffed Roasted Pheasant Legs Crêpinette); two of the watercress-based offerings were the result of one chef's highly unpleasant encounter with ducks (Watercress Salad with Duck Tongues, Watercress Salad with Duck Testicles). Jean-Louis Palladin ordered fifteen hundred shiners from the local bait shop and made Shiners Tempura; said a local who attends the dinner, "We haven't looked at our bait bucket the same since."

But it is the traditional first main course of the night that dominates the festivities. "Here they are, guys," announces Perona Farms proprietor Wade Avondoglio at about seven-thirty P.M. each year. "Get in line for the woodcock heads," whereupon, using a wax candle, he proceeds to roast the golfball-sized heads of a number of woodcocks, dip them in a veal glaze, slice the crowns of their heads off, and then hand them to diners by the birds' large beak. "You put it in your mouth and just suck out those delicious little brains," Avondoglio said, "and the eyes, too, if you want to."

As Matt Dillon noted, "Excellent grub."

=

"How was everything?" Balegh the busboy asked us as we lingered at the table in our postpayment, predeparture mode.

"Oh, it was great," I said. "The food was great."

"We loved it," Erica murmured.

"Yes—thank you," I added.

"Good, good," he responded.

He reached down to brush a few crumbs off the table, saying, "I would like now to take you on a tour of the dining room."

WHAT IF YOUR CLEANING WOMAN BECAME
A DOCUMENTARY FILMMAKER?

First Visit   Cleaning woman leaves all your family portraits face down in defiant protest of staged action.

Second Visit   Cleaning woman takes vacuum attachment off base: decision to go "hand-held" proves influential to her aesthetic.

Third Visit   Cleaning woman says her last film liberated Janitor from Drum.

Fourth Visit   Cleaning woman shoots new work of verité, *Shoe Tree: A Portrait.*

Fifth Visit   Cleaning woman records depressing Bach fugue to lay over *Shoe Tree* visuals.

Sixth Visit   Cleaning woman dons mules and stained negligee for undercover exposé of local brothel.

Seventh Visit   Cleaning woman explains she is cutting back hours due to additional funding from Mobil.

WHAT IF SOCIAL CLIMBING WERE
A FORM OF RELIGION?

First Rite   Climber asks that discovery of his name in *Town and Country* be followed by moment of silence.

Second Rite   Climber buys indulgence after forgetting to have himself paged during meeting in lobby of Waldorf.

Third Rite   Climber tithes to boarding school's alumni magazine.

Fourth Rite   Recently arrested climber invokes intercession of saintlike "friend," a partner at Cravath, Swaine & Moore.

Fifth Rite   Climber takes unintentional vow of chastity: spends entire cocktail party without telling anyone he knew Meryl and Wendy at Yale.

WHAT IF MR. PEANUT RAN A STRIP JOINT CALLED "THE PARTY MIX"?

9:50 P.M. Candee Pecan lifts part of shell provocatively; customers scream, "Shell it!"

10:24 P.M. Mr. P. introduces Whata Chestnut as "a tempest in a D-cup."

12:02 A.M. Mr. P. tells new cage dancer that pretzel-customers will do "anything for titty."

12:35 A.M. Bouncer removes raisin who has attached himself to Almond Joy.

1:04 A.M. Topless Beechnut commences novelty wrestling by entering creamed-corn pit.

1:27 A.M. Honey-slathered peanut-dancer smolders under harsh spotlight in climactic throes of the Honey Roast.

2:20 A.M. Miss Macadamia starts rumor that her competitor sleeps in dirt.

3:44 A.M. Mr. Salty and other pretzels arrive; Mr. P. runs into dressing room, shouts, "Fleet's in!"

4:30 A.M. Mr. P. removes top hat and monocle; saunters out to parking lot to fellate Brazil nut.

The Egg and Me

She was white-haired and soft-spoken, and she was a poet. You could tell her hair color by looking and her timbre by listening, but her status as a poet—a subtler thing—was best revealed by her presence in the ballroom of the Washington, D.C., Hilton, where she was joining two thousand fellow award-winning poets—many of them also soft-spoken, white-haired ladies—at the fifth annual World of Poetry convention.

Of course, her avocation was also revealed by what she was saying to a small circle of newfound friends about the verses she composed when the space shuttle Challenger crashed. "When I sat down to write," she said, "the words just flowed." As she told the story the corners of her eyes glistened with tears. Her husband, sitting next to her, put his arm on her shoulder comfortingly. "Yep, that was a good one," he said, beaming with pride. "I had that one *laminated.*"

=

Not all of the conventioneers were feeling similarly loved. Upon their arrival at the Hilton that afternoon, several of the people new to the World of Poetry—a Sacramento-based organization that, according to its founder, John Campbell, has more than 1.1 million members and is the largest poetry society in the world—made an unsettling discovery. Having entered a poetry contest advertised in publications ranging from *The Atlantic* to *USA Today* and having received an exuberant letter of congratulations that invited them to the convention ("I'm so excited to tell you the good news! World of Poetry's board of directors has voted unanimously to honor you with our Golden Poet Award for 1989, in recognition of your poem, which you entered in our Free Poetry Contest. What is the Golden Poet Award? . . . The Golden Poet Award is to poets what the Academy Award is to actors"), many of them arrived under the impression that they alone had won.

But the World of Poetry is not a cruel, Hobbesian world in which a single winner has vanquished many lesser worthies in his dog-eat-dog climb to the top. No, no, no. The World of Poetry is a kind world, a loving world. There was not *one* winner. There were *two thousand.*

Those Golden Poets—along with anyone who bothered to respond at all—were offered the opportunity to come to

Washington at their own expense, enter a poem in the convention contest, and contend for thirty-five thousand dollars in cash and prizes and the World of Poetry poet laureateship. Some, like the frankly disappointed woman from North Carolina who had forgone paying her car insurance for a month in order to attend, decided simply to "chalk this one up to experience." Others felt more pointedly aggrieved. But to prove how loving a world the World of Poetry is, the hosts reimbursed, out of the approximately $1.7 million they had raked in, any conventioneer who felt cheated (the poets had paid a $495 fee, their guests, $425). A square deal, yes, perhaps even a loving one; still, you could not help but feel sorry for people like Elaine Martin, a woman with cerebral palsy whose friends and relatives had held a fund-raiser so that she and her sister could come from Cincinnati, or Priya Sharma, a young woman whose parents had paid for her flight from Bhopal, India.

=

The weekend-long convention was a veritable shivaree of events. Upon registering, the two thousand soon-to-be award-winning poets, along with their guests and numerous non-award-winning poets, were treated to an hour-long "Gala Champagne Reception," followed by a "Gala Afternoon Welcome." The emphasis, it seemed, was on the gala. Of the twenty-seven scheduled hours of the convention, only five and a half could be construed as poetry oriented—an hour and a half on "oral interpretation" and a four-hour period during which all the poets split into smaller groups and read their work to one another.

Much of the convention was devoted to gushy show-biz acts and shameless self-congratulation, the prime practitioner of which was World of Poetry editor and publisher John Campbell, who had himself been crowned laureate of the first convention, in 1985. Campbell's Saturday-night performance, advertised as a "one-man Shakespearean explosion!" proved to be the perfect showcase for the coy, roly-poly Campbell, who donned period costume and tested the audience's memory of the nursery rhyme "Little Miss Muffet." ("Let's give ourselves a hand for that!") Then he sat on a golden throne and read Lewis Carroll's "The Walrus and the Carpenter" while the pedestal of the throne spewed, in classic Elizabethan fashion, a large cloud of soap bubbles.

Other speakers included Bob Hope, Jayne Meadows (who at one point asked the audience, "Aren't I *marvelous*?"), poet Sonia Sanchez, and American poet laureate Howard Nemerov—yes, the *real* poet laureate. Four other celebrity poetry buffs who were advertised did not show: Helen Hayes, Tony Randall, Willard Scott, and poet Louis Simpson. Campbell made various excuses for their absence; but, according to *The Washington Post* and *The Washington Times*, darker forces had prevailed: All four had backed out upon finding out more about the World of Poetry. According to the *Times*, an agent at Helen Hayes's agency called the convention "a scandal," and the *Post* quoted Louis

Simpson as saying it was "a rip-off." Nemerov—the most prestigious speaker booked for the convention—came to the conclusion that the convention was "technically legal, but not kosher," and tried to get out of the engagement but was contractually bound. "As I can't get out of it," he said, "I'll go in with a good heart, a clean mouth, and will keep a civil tongue in my cheek. . . . It's more like P. T. Barnum than Hitler, you know."

But no matter who appeared, the audience—which, to be fair, was primarily composed of happy people returning to the convention for their second or third time—responded warmly; in the course of fifteen scheduled hours in the ballroom, no fewer than seven standing ovations were given. For many, the proceedings were an emotional whirligig, a chance to wallow in pronouncements like "We are all poets."

Nevertheless, several of the poets I talked to were dismayed by the quality of the poetry that had been recognized. "Anybody could throw words together and they got an award for it," one poet complained. "Compared with what I've heard at other poetry readings, this stuff is disgusting."

It did seem that an awful lot of, well, *chaff* had been produced by these Golden Poets. I wondered how bad a poem had to be to preclude its being recognized. With this in mind, I hastily penned the following:

I Am in the Egg; Hello! Hello!

Orblike within my shell,
I am a sticky placenta beach ball

I am yolkness
I am *of* yolk
Yolk yolk yolk
Yolks for sale!
    (I'll take two, they're small)
I am trapped inside a gigantic rubber egg
Please help me.

When I read this poem to my fellow conventioneers, it was
met with great acclaim. "This is great," one young man
raved. Another, who had won his invitation to the convention with his "Sonnet in Sympathy with Exploited Labor in
South America," said, "Deep, esoteric—it's wonderful.
Sometimes the realization of our own insignificance keeps
us within our own shell." A similar grasp of theme was
manifested by Jeanny Losey, the sixty-four-year-old Indiana
housewife who had bagged the twelve-thousand-dollar
grand prize and the poet laureateship in 1986. "Yes," she
responded, after considering the poem at length. "It seems
like we always feel like we're closed in."

Having been praised thusly, I set out in search of John
Campbell to receive the ultimate validation, but he had, like
one of his throne's bubbles, suddenly vanished. I settled for
the teary Catherine McCord, who had just finished serving
as one of three judges of the fifteen-thousand-dollar grand
prize and the poet laureateship. Although it was too late to
get my ovatic masterpiece into the contest, it wasn't too late
to get a little helpful feedback. McCord was up on the
stage, next to the judges' table, hovering on the periphery

of postcoronation hysteria. I mounted the stage and squirmed through the crowd and read my poem to her. Slowly and meaningfully. She paused. She coughed. Suspense mounted. Finally, out it came: "It's wonderful. I love it. It's beautifully *crafted.*"

And soon to be beautifully laminated as well.

MOVING ON

Dread and Breakfast

The visitor to Manhattan who is in search of accommodations that might be billed as "inexpensive but lovely"
is faced with a dearth of possibilities—hotels are rarely the
former; the YMCA never the latter. Thus it was with a sense
of epiphany and joy that I opened the Manhattan Yellow
Pages and discovered, sandwiched between "Bed Boards"
and "Bed Frames (Metal)" a section entitled "Bed and
Breakfast" with some fifteen entries.

Those who have traveled Europe or back-roads America
and who have stayed at bed and breakfasts are well ac-
quainted with the pleasures and enchantments that result
when natives with a surfeit of square footage open their
homes and their hearts to weary travelers. The paying guest
in a stranger's home is also aware of what the typical B & B
lacks—pool privileges, tiny guest soaps, a room down the
hall with several hundred pounds of free ice. No, the words

bed and breakfast are synonymous with homelike charm, with four-posters and counterpanes and a gift jar of the hostess's own blackberry jam, with clapboard houses on winding lanes and afternoon tea round the fire. Sunrise Farm, Hill & Hollow, Breezy Acres Farm, the Burton House, the Inn at Fordhook Farm, Ashley Manor—the names themselves betoken old-fashioned country comfort and delight.

And yet . . . and yet . . . happy as I was to learn that New York City, improbably, had bed and breakfasts, I was forced to ask myself whether they could provide the kind of spirit-lifting loveliness and warm human touch for which bed and breakfasts are known. Breezy Acres on West Twenty-third Street? The Inn at Fordhook on upper Broadway? I wondered.

My curiosity piqued, I set out to visit some bed and breakfasts in New York City with the hope of answering these questions:

1. Would my hosts eventually untie me and allow me to live?
2. Would I really be served breakfast?

Most travelers find Manhattan B & Bs through reservation services, of which there are at least ten. One calls a service, explains for what night and in what neighborhood one is looking for accommodations, and then answers questions as to whether or not one is able to endure cigarette smoke, more than two flights of stairs, pets, or shared bathrooms. Of course, suspicion has no place in this cozy world. None of the three services I used asked me to meet them or provide references. All they knew, and all my hosts knew, was that I was male and probably in my twenties—the precise profile of the typical violent felon.

I stayed at a handful of different bed and breakfasts in Manhattan. I asked to stay at the least expensive ones in the city, and made no demands about smoking, pets, stairs, or anything else. The price per night ran between sixty and eighty dollars, for which the reservation service takes a cut of about 25 percent. (The price for a night at a typical hotel in New York is about twice that.) My hosts said they averaged around six guests a month; and so they all had real jobs in addition to welcoming complete strangers into their homes and offering them toast.

I learned many things from my experience. I learned that even in the big, anonymous city, people are reaching out to people. And I learned that these people are very strange.

UPPER WEST SIDE STORY
Pussy Willows and Suspect Soap

An elfin woman in her early sixties who wears her hair in bangs bids me enter her dark apartment on the Upper West Side, takes my bag, and immediately and awkwardly says, "Let me show you your room." The room is small and dark and is defined on the top by a swirly stucco ceiling and on the bottom by two pieces of carpet that are both beginning to unravel. A Coke bottle filled with dried pussywillows sits on a drab wooden dresser. My host suggests that I get myself settled and then come join her in the kitchen.

As I am unpacking I notice that the transom over the door to my room has been knocked out, and suddenly I am glad that my plans for the evening do not involve having sex. I am moved, however, to check the bed linens, and I discover that they are floral-printed and are actually transparent in parts. "I could probably read *The New York Times* through these!" I think, aware that this is an accolade for croissant dough, not for bedsheets.

Moments later I walk down the hall, an area illuminated, as my room is, by naked overhead bulbs, and I pass the bathroom and another guest bedroom before entering the kitchen. The kitchen appears to be a repository for cat postcards and dried flowers and dead plants in La Yogurt containers. Its floor is clad in a hazy coffee-nougat-phlegm-colored linoleum that in one spot has begun to buckle. I join my host at the kitchen table, and we talk for about forty-five minutes, during which time she emerges as an intelligent and energetic chain-smoker. Shortly into our talk, I bring up the topic of money and say, "Should I pay you now or should I w—" whereupon, pupils practically blazing with holographic dollar signs, she cuts me off with "Why don't we get it over with now?" Her intensity resurfaces later in the conversation when she presses her finger against the red plastic tablecloth and, pinpointing a crumb, gingerly places the crumb in her mouth and swallows. I now realize that the unkempt nature of the apartment is less a reflection of lack of effort than it is of this rather time-consuming cleaning process.

When I get up to go out for dinner, my host lays out a few of the ground plans. There will be coffee, tea, and bagels on the table in the morning, and I am to help myself to them. I am free to sit in the kitchen as much as I want. There will be a couple staying in the second bedroom; my host herself will be staying with her visiting brother in the closed-off front part of the apartment. "We like to leave the bathroom door open when no one is using it," she also explains, "so no one gets stuck in the hall wondering whether or not it's okay to knock."

The next morning I am awakened by the sound of the two other guests and my host in the kitchen. Not wanting to have to interact in my precaffeinated state, I loll in bed until it sounds as though they have left the kitchen. A cursory glance around the room reveals that I have been provided with a respectable bath towel; an old but not yet fraying flesh-colored handcloth; and a sad, black-and-yellow-plaid washcloth possibly dating from the Eisenhower administration. I pad down to the bathroom, witness its grout deterioration, am vaguely repulsed by the sight of human hair and used Q-Tips in the unemptied trash can there, and decide to brave a shower. The unwrapped bar of soap in the shower looks newish but not brand spanking new; I put it between my clenched hands and lather off a good quarter inch of its potentially pubic-hair-afflicted surface before applying it to my person.

Later, once dressed, I walk out of my room, whereupon

my host, dressed in a nubbly, bright red bunny-type sleep-ing garment, materializes in the hallway and appears anxious to make me coffee. I tell her that I am going out to buy the paper; she oddly responds, "Oh, are you leaving now?" I tell her no, I am simply going to buy the paper and then I will be right back. This reiteration of my agenda seems to sink in, and she asks if it would be okay if she strips the bed while I am gone. I give this proposal my ready assent.

When I return, the apartment is eerily quiet. The other guests have left and I cannot find my host. With a sense of slightly anxious peacefulness, I sit in the kitchen, which is lit by a single fluorescent bulb over the sink, and drink some coffee and eat a bagel and read the paper. I've had the bed and now—breakfast!

Thirty minutes or so later, I pack and seek out my host. I knock on the door of her part of the apartment; her brother greets me and tells me she is out doing laundry, so I thank him and leave. The polite hemisphere of my brain wonders momentarily if I am meant to tip my host, but then the impolite hemisphere sniggers at the very idea.

VILLAGE VISIT
Spaciousness and a Surprise

The second apartment I stay at is in Greenwich Village, an area noted for its bed-and-breakfasty charm. The apartment features a huge living room that separates my room from the kitchen. However, my host, a vivacious, zaftig single woman in her early sixties, makes no mention of whether the living room lies within my purlieu, and thus this unavoidable area taunts me throughout the rest of my stay like a large, throbbing question mark. She does, however, make clear that I will once again share a bathroom with another guest. I accept this news with stoicism.

Uncertain of my permitted range, I confine myself mostly to my room, a twelve-by-fifteen-foot box lit by an overhead bulb shaded by what looks like a crocheted cap with tassels—perhaps an early prototype for the Shriners' fez. The door to the room, in addition to having a one-inch clearance from the floor, has a two-by-three-foot section of shutters in it, thus ensuring maximum noise carryover. At one point, while I am purposefully headed to the bathroom, my host introduces me to the other guest—a businessman from Michigan who, because he has a lot of work in Manhattan, has reserved a room with the host for Tuesday through Thursday for the entire month. The enthusiasm that the host expresses for the other guest ("A regular! All the way from Michigan!") makes me feel like a younger, less-loved sibling.

When I return from dinner that night, I can hear the news from the TV in my host's bedroom, yet she emerges from the kitchen. She tells me that she likes to listen to the news while she exercises—an activity that I can only imagine involves a lot of crouching and lotion. She walks into her bedroom, so I take the opportunity to glance briefly at some of the artwork in the outer area of the living room, still tantalizing, still unapproachable.

Later that night at around ten o'clock I decide to go outside for a walk. I grab the spare house key my host has provided me and walk out of my room. Nothing could have prepared me for what I then witness; for there, traipsing across the living room on her way to the kitchen, is my host, her calves and fleshy lower thighs unprotected by the scant yardage of her T-shirt-style nightie. In an effort to mask my nervous laughter I produce a sound that is somewhere between coughing, strangling, and revving a large outboard motor. I avert my eyes from my host's and scurry out the door.

The next morning, while I am sitting at the dining room table and enjoying my rather lavish, tasty, serve-yourself breakfast (bagels, English and blueberry muffins, coffee or tea), my host walks out of her bedroom dressed in work clothes and informs me that she has to be at work at nine but that I can stay. I thank her for her hospitality and tell her that I will leave the key on the dining room table.

Shortly after her departure I enter the living room, and I lounge victoriously on the couch for twenty minutes before heading to my office.

MIDTOWN NOCTURNE
"The Moonlight Affects Me . . . Strangely"

"Come on in. But why don't you take your shoes off," says my third host, a beatific, lovely woman in her late forties wearing a loose, tie-dyed jumpsuit. "We don't wear shoes here. This is a sanctuary." I oblige her request, walk into her immaculate midtown apartment, and behold three women lounging on the floor of the living room. It is a large, minimalist room, its whiteness punctuated only by three Turneresque paintings, two wire sculptures, a grand piano, two small chairs, and an ottoman.

I pick up my bag and ask her if I might put it in my room. She looks at me quizzically, pauses, and then, pointing to the right, says, "You'll either be in here—which is my bedroom—or in the living room on a futon. Or out on the terrace if you would like." In deference to my own personal safety, I opt for the living room.

My host introduces me to her three friends and then says, "Just make yourself comfortable. They won't be here *all* night," a statement that I find unsettling, given that the women are currently sprawled on the floor of what is to be my sleeping quarters.

I am invited to join them, so I hover briefly on the periphery of their group. They are eating chips and salsa and reading to one another from a spiritual book called *Being a Woman: Fulfilling Your Femininity and Finding Love,* and then relating the passages to their own lives. Not being a woman, I find my attention lapses and I wander out onto the terrace. Several moments later my host comes out and asks if I would like to sit out there in a chair; I say yes and she brings me a very comfortable folding deck chair. Then she goes back into the apartment and returns with a folded-up piece of fabric that she hands to me saying, "Here is a sarong. You can just slip into it. We aren't bashful here."

However, I *am*, so once she has turned and gone back into the apartment, I reach over the doorsill and lay the sarong on the living room floor. I sit and try to relax. I look at the sarong. I think, *What?*

When I go back inside an hour or so later, I discover that my host has moved my bag onto a massage table in her bedroom. I put my sneakers on and walk into the living room in order to tell her that I am going out for dinner, whereupon she stares at my sneakers and chastises me for the "negative energy" that they might unleash in her apartment.

Once outside, resentful that aspersions have been cast on my footwear, I avenge myself by going to a restaurant and eating a lot of meat.

When I return to the apartment, I slip off my shoes and enter to find that the three women have left but a new one has arrived. She and the host and I go out on the terrace and marvel at the nearly full moon. My host sets up a futon on the floor of the living room for me and explains that her bed is also portable. Then she says, "I may bring it out here and come join you. I tend to wander about in the night." I smile bleakly.

A few minutes later I follow her into her bedroom to get a pillow, and she takes the opportunity to say to me, "Don't be bashful around me."

"Don't be bashful about *what?*" I ask.

"Don't be bashful about me because I'm not bashful around you."

About an hour later her guest leaves, and twenty minutes

after that I get into bed, sure that I will awaken in the middle of the night and find myself being either raped or shaved.

The following morning, however, I arise intact and un-scathed. I notice that my bag has been moved from the massage table in the bedroom into the hall. After dressing hurriedly and self-consciously in the bathroom, I am treated to a wonderful breakfast of plain and chocolate croissants, slices of melon and freshly brewed coffee. During this repast my host and I get to talking about owning things, and she says, "I don't believe in ownership. I think that I have a part of all things and all things are a part of me." I ask my host what she would do if a friend of hers were wearing a shirt that my host knew would flatter her more than her friend. My host replies that she would either ask the friend where she got the shirt or she would say, "You have had that shirt long enough and maybe I should have it for a while."

I instinctively clutch my bag, and a short while thereafter, my bag and I leave.

EAST SIDE ELEGANCE
Helpful Hints and Thoughts About Cheese

My next stay, in the East Nineties, distinguishes itself on two counts: a) the host is a male; b) he offers a snack service.

On the bedside table in my room I find a mimeographed note. "Hi," it reads. "Welcome to your home away from home. I am pleased to have you as a guest and would like you to enjoy your stay. How can I help you? Do you need information about sightseeing? transportation? entertainment? Just ask. If I don't know, I'll be glad to find out for you. Do you need an ironing board? A hair dryer? Would you care for a snack before you retire? All are available upon request. (The evening snack service is $3.50 additional to your room rate.) Breakfast will be served between 7 A.M. and 8 A.M. If that time is not convenient for your schedule, and you prefer to serve yourself at a later time, please make arrangements with me before you retire. If you need to be in and out during the day, a house key is available so you can let yourself in and out as you please. You are welcome to join us in the family room for television any evening after 8 P.M. A small radio is available for use in your room if you wish. Laundry equipment is available for your use at [Wite-Out blotch] charge. You will find extra blankets and towels on the upper shelf of your closet, should you need them. Please let me know anything I can do to make yours a very pleasant stay." I think the note is admirably comprehensive.

I don't partake of the snack service, but over breakfast the next morning (coffee, four pieces of bakery-fresh white bread, a pot of marmalade, a pot of margarine) I chat with my host—a large, bespectacled man in his fifties—about it. It is favored largely by his younger clientele. "They don't eat enough dinner, they need more. [I give them] cold cuts. An egg, a soft-boiled egg. Cheese—I keep a lot of cheese around. Or a sandwich." When he mentions the cheese, the way he says *around* faintly suggests that he uses the word literally. The rest of my stay is marked by an unshakable expectation that I will encounter cheese in some inappropriate setting.

PARTIAL PARK VIEW PLEASURES
Midway, More Soap, and An Act of Aggression

When it comes time to stay at my last Manhattan bed and breakfast, I recall the words of Bernice Chesler, as I often do in my private moments. Miss Chesler is the travel philosopher and author of *Bed and Breakfast in the Mid-Atlantic States,* among other works. With regard to the bed and breakfast, she has written that "the keynote is hospitality" and that it is "a people-to-people program." I realize that by remaining in my room too much at night and tending to avoid the living areas, I have failed to test these principles. I am now determined to become more of a people person.

My final host lives on the West Side near Central Park. She is a small, peppy woman in her early sixties, and she shows me directly to my room without mentioning her large living room. I am now a man with a mission.

I return from dinner to find that my host has gone out shopping (as she told me earlier she would) and that all the lights in the living room and adjoining dining area are off. I turn on a lamp in the living room and pull a chair up to the television. I turn the TV on and discover that the war classic *Midway* is being shown on channel five. I turn up the volume so that the soundtrack adequately mimics a sea battle.

When my host returns about twenty minutes later, she looks in on me with an initial air of distraction and confusion. But seconds later, sporting an apparently genuine smile, she asks me what I am watching. When I reply that it is *Midway*, she does not seem enthusiastic and goes into the kitchen to unpack her groceries.

Several minutes later she comes back into the living room. "I finally got some *soap*!" she says triumphantly, apparently unaware of the relative ease with which we others find and buy this product. She has bought a five-pack of Ivory and, while extolling the virtues of its subtle fragrance, encourages me to smell a bar. I do, but then quickly return to *Midway*. As the pace of the fiery maelstrom of warfare and combat starts to quicken, I decide to cheer on the battle scenes. "Bah-*bing*!" I say when a bomb is dropped on an American ship; when a Japanese plane erupts in flames I cheer, *"Bingo!"* My host looks at me slightly askance, chuckles nervously, and remarks that the *depiction* of war is so much less frightening than actual war. She then goes and sits on the couch behind me and noisily reads *The New York Times*.

At ten o'clock I stand and switch the channel to PBS, which is airing *Metamorphosis: Man into Woman*, a documentary about a man who has a sex change. My host and I watch this with rapt curiosity. When she is forced to answer the phone twice during the show, she appears slightly vexed and hurries the callers off the line.

I decide to go further. I want to see how the people-to-people program really works. Over breakfast the next morning I lie elaborately, telling my host that I am a decorator and that I have recently graduated from a community college in Massachusetts with a degree in interior design. She seems genuinely interested and asks me several questions about my schooling. Shortly thereafter I pack my bag and thank my host for her hospitality. Then, bag in hand, I tell my host that I have *rethought* the arrangement of some of the furniture in the room that I slept in. She titters nervously and expectantly and asks to see. I open the door to the bedroom and allow her eyes to take in the changes that I wrought before going to bed the night before. I have moved the queen-size bed four inches to the left, moved the dark pine Swedish modern desk fifteen feet or so across the room to where the bedside table was (and put the bedside table where the desk was), and I have switched the positions of the two framed posters.

She takes one look and says, "Oh, it's *nice*. It looks . . . it really looks nice."

"Oh, you don't mind it?" I say with feigned modesty. "I completely understand if you hate it. It's just that it's so hard for me to spend time in a space and not *interact* with it, even on the most minimal level. I didn't move *all* the pieces."

Noticing the open area created by the exchange of the

largish desk for the smaller bedside table, she says, "Oooh—it certainly makes it easier to get in here to the bathroom."

"Yes," I say, picking up her lead. "I think it really opens up the space. I was trying to create . . . *egress.*"

"Ahh," she says, apparently trying to digest this particular design element.

I walk out into the hallway, eager to leave. She accompanies me and, on our way to the door, titters, "It's *nifty* what you did in there. Oh yes, that's something."

Two days later, under the pretext of having lost a contact lens during my stay, I return to the apartment and discover that the furniture remains the way I arranged it. My host mentions that she spent the night in the guest room.

"You slept in *this* room?" I ask incredulously.

"Well, I was just concerned that with the desk so close to the bed now that it might be a little cramped, but it's not. It's good if you want to do some writing or use the desk. I really like it! I like spaciousness and this way is much more spacious."

I feel complete. I feel *loved.* But then, suddenly: "I've got some spare furniture in *my* bedroom, too; *but I'm not going to show it to you.*"

=

My sojourns at the homes of total strangers are behind me now. And although I cannot say that I have forged any new friendships or that I plan to invite any of my hosts to my own home, I have come to learn more about New York, more about my needs as a guest, and, yes, perhaps a little more about myself. In the past, my behavior in cities has always been guided by three simple maxims: Don't talk to strangers. Look both ways before crossing. Don't sleep in the subway, darling. Now, having paid to stay at several of Manhattan's homiest accommodations, I know that it is important not to be bashful around strangers, because they are not bashful around me.

WHAT IF A DEBUTANTE'S FOREHEAD
WERE SUDDENLY STAMPED "CARGO"?

Darien, Conn.	**Trucker wishes that debutantes came with large wooden handles.**
New York, N.Y.	**Longshoreman bemoans debutante's big "keester" and noticeable dearth of "nay-nays."**
Indianapolis, Ind.	**Debutante inhales fumes from front-end loader; hallucinates that she is married to her horse, Black Misty.**
New York, N.Y.	**Debutante sends notecard to her friends, Boo-Boo and Icky.**
Darien, Conn.	**Debutante tells trucker to let her know if there's anything she needs to sign for.**

WHAT IF RALPH LAUREN DESIGNED COMPUTER VIRUSES INSTEAD OF CLOTHING?

"Surrey" Virus inserts word *quite* before all of text's adjectives.

"Taos" Screen is filled with stripes and patterns of endless Navajo blanket.

"Jockey" All characters are reduced to ⅓ their normal size.

"Tailgate Picnic" Printer spews cloud of deviled eggs and exhaust fumes.

"Gatwick" Text circles screen for hours; comes out printer with portions lost.

"Old Money" Characters cavort around screen drunkenly; disappear until following day at noon.

**WHAT IF THE CAST OF *THE MCLAUGHLIN GROUP*
WERE LIVING INSIDE YOUR BATHROOM?**

8:30 A.M.   Fred tells Pat he disagrees: creme rinse does
              not result in more volume.

8:31 A.M.   Group discusses whether Tidy Bowl Man
              should be granted political asylum.

8:33 A.M.   McLaughlin terrorizes Eleanor with towel
              snapping and soap horns.

8:35 A.M.   Replenishing of toilet paper launches
              debate: over or under?

10:47 P.M.   Jack lurks lasciviously near drain with
              blowsy Scrubbing Bubble.

11:03 P.M.   Fred's tub-and-basin-region prediction
              provokes fiery exchange about Zud.

Foreign Objects (How to Translate Your Foreign Lover)

It is inevitable that those of us who are of artistic leaning will, at some point during our urban residency, consort with foreigners. Entering international waters in the hope that some of our foreign friends' sophistication and passive involvement in the history of culture and civilization will rub off on us, we the domestic party seek a streamlined form of education: travel without the inconvenience of travel.

That these relationships are fraught with miscommunication and misunderstanding is not unrelated to why we got involved with a foreigner in the first place—after all, liaisons with foreigners offer nothing if not the swank of incompatibility. But before long, the relationship's peculiar charm begins to wane, and we realize that we are as moths attracted to a flame: Before you can inform your British lover of the whereabouts of your guest towels, he has inventoried your liquor cabinet and arranged a "drinks party" for his friend Natasha, the Belts and Accessories Editor at *Vogue;* before you can figure out what has upset your Russian lover, he is sobbing in a foreign language and arranging for his funeral to be held in Minsk.

The dire state that these relationships can reach is best evidenced by Zsa Zsa Gabor, the Hungarian author of *How to Catch a Man, How to Keep a Man, How to Get Rid of a Man.* Several years ago, my friend Bob Mack, then a fact-checker at *Spy* magazine, was asked to call Miss Gabor in order to verify the dates of her marriage to her sixth husband, an American named Jack Ryan. We pick up Bob's notes just as Miss Gabor surfaces:

ZSA ZSA: Hello, dahling. I just love your magazine, it's wonderful!

BOB: Well, thank you, ma'am, that's very kind of you. I'm sorry to intrude, but I'm fact-checking this story and I need to find out the exact dates of when you were married to Jack Ryan.

ZSA ZSA: Dahling, I was never married to Jack Ryan! I love that man, he was wonderful, a brilliant inventor, but I never married him.

BOB: Umm, the way I understand it, you married him in 1975.

(At this point, Bob was looking at Miss Gabor's entry in *Who's Who,* which, although it stated that Mr. Ryan became Miss Gabor's sixth husband in 1975, gave no divorce date.)

ZSA ZSA: Oh no, dahling! Jack lived right down the street from me. He was a wonderful man, always throwing parties in his tree house. I loved him. My husband, Mr. Rubirosa, Porfirio Rubirosa, was very jealous. I loved Jack, but I never married him.

(Stifled, Bob then dutifully listened to Miss Gabor prattle on about a number of topics, including the $2 million advance that Delacorte Press had given her to write her autobiography. Just as Bob was summoning up his courage to ask his question one more time, she blurted out:)

ZSA ZSA: Oh, dahling, you're right! I *was* married to Jack Ryan! He's such a wonderful man.

Lest, like Mr. Ryan, we allow the small misunderstandings of our relationships with foreigners to pile up to the point of total bafflement, I offer the useful guide that begins on the next page.

When Your ITALIAN Lover Says:	*What Your ITALIAN Lover* MEANS *Is:*
"You are a very kind man."	"Marry my sister."
"What a charming studio apartment."	"But where will you put Mamma and Cousin Giacinta?"

When Your BRITISH Lover Says:	*What Your BRITISH Lover* MEANS *Is:*
"You enjoy the distinction of being, as it were, paramount in our affections."	"I am wonderful."
"The manner in which you camouflage your inner pain with daft enthusiasm is quite refreshing."	"You are Liza Minnelli."

When Your GERMAN Lover Says:	*What Your GERMAN Lover* MEANS *Is:*
"I have taken many photographs of my hometown's iron foundries and dams."	"I have taken many photographs of my hometown's iron foundries and dams."

When Your JAPANESE Lover Says:	*What Your JAPANESE Lover MEANS Is:*
"There has always been a mythic, larger-than-life quality to Americans for me."	"Could you reach that box of cereal on the top shelf for me?"

When Your HUNGAR-IAN Lover Says:	*What Your HUNGAR-IAN Lover MEANS Is:*
"Words cannot express the utter rapture that I feel in your presence."	"Dahling—have we met?"

When Your MOLDA-VIAN Lover Says:	*What Your MOLDA-VIAN Lover MEANS Is:*
"Thank you."	"A pair of shoes! With a *buckle*!"

When Your FRENCH Lover Says:	*What Your FRENCH Lover MEANS Is:*
"I hate you!"	"Where are my cigarettes?!"
"I detest you!"	"Where are my cigarettes?!"

"Leave at once!"

"I do love you, darling. It's simply that we are essentially so different—I enjoy carrying on several simultaneous affairs with my bisexual cousins; you enjoy *Roseanne*.

"But thank God for those opportunities when I can laugh at you and your clothing. This striped shirt is particularly amusing—I am reminded of my childhood fascination with clowns.

"But cheri, be a love, won't you—Marlboros. In a box."

WHAT IF YOUR MOTHER WERE A FORM OF INTERACTIVE MEDIA?

Monday MOM boots up to opening bars of favorite Neil Diamond song.

Tuesday MOM interrupts banking program with unsolicited virtual reality tour, "Adorable Herb Gardens and Bird Sanctuaries I Have Visited with Your Father."

Wednesday Memo from local cable system warns subscribers of likelihood that MOM will malfunction during holidays.

Thursday MOM interfaces with neighbor's system for downloading and coffee.

Friday MOM says that your hilarious woes of interactivity would make a wonderful Erna Bombank column.

Saturday MOM translates sentiment "As long as you have your health" into a binary series of on-off electronic impulses.

Sunday Sudden increase of interactive shopping programs causes MOM to crash, transmit virus.

WHAT IF MICHELANGELO HAD BEEN HETEROSEXUAL?

1508 Michelangelo stares at mistake made in mural, hoping for sudden appearance of slo-mo instant replay.

1509 Michelangelo replaces Sistine Chapel's sibyls and prophets with photos of José Canseco and Kathy Ireland.

1510 Michelangelo and friends blow past the Medici Palace on bitchin' two-wheeled wagons.

1513 Michelangelo reworks sketch for sculpture *Dying Slave* as *Slave Guy: Keep on Truckin'*.

1514 Michelangelo's unveiling of statue causes friends to do the Wave.

1519 Michelangelo likens allegorical sculptures *Dawn, Dusk, Day,* and *Night* to a Girls of the Big Ten pictorial.

1523 Michelangelo develops interest in barbecuing and lawn care.

1530 Michelangelo's winning of bet earns him opportunity to throw one free punch at Pope Clement.

WHAT IF YOUR TRAVEL AGENT
WENT OFF LITHIUM?

First Travel agent suggests tour, "Around the World in Three Days."

Then Travel agent suggests tour, "Albania: Land of Sorrow."

First Travel agent organizes window display featuring bratwurst and dirndls.

Then Travel agent organizes window display featuring broken glass and first-aid kits.

First Travel agent sends thirteen brochures about Carnaval in Rio.

Then Travel agent sends tattered paperback of *Death in Venice.*

Beauty Through Science

Because I am five-ten and have looks more evocative of the works of Norman Rockwell than those of Giorgio Armani, I have never given much thought to the possibility of becoming a male model. However, when a colleague pointed out to me in the spring of 1993 that, given the unidealized nature of beauty then being found in the media—the underfed waifs, the grizzled beatniks, the drowsy androgynes—men no longer had to be hulks in order to be awarded lucrative modeling contracts, I suddenly realized that it was entirely possible that *even I,* with my bony frame, could be making a profit simply by posing. So I went to my bathroom mirror and savored the possibility that I might finally get to *know* the Milan airport. My moment, I sensed, was near—the moment I would walk into a modeling agency and have a large woman in a muu-muu pinch my cheek and gasp, "Ten pounds of gorgeous in a five-pound bag!"

=

But before I could go to modeling agencies and gauge the salability of my own decidedly unidealized, unchiseled looks, before I could tilt at the hydra of humiliation and rejection, I had to put together a "book"—a portfolio of photographs capturing my dizzying range of looks and attitudes.

I met with a photographer and stylist recommended by a friend. The two men's level of hipness was discomfitting: the stylist wore a lot of rumpled black clothing and a crocheted skullcap; the photographer wore an earring and leather bell-bottoms. "I'm not sure how you'll photograph," the photographer said, gazing at me skeptically. I showed them some professional portraits I had had taken a month earlier by a photographer who takes a lot of actors' headshots; the duo was unimpressed. (Photographer: "They're very Broadway." Stylist: *"Very* Broadway.")

"How's the body?" asked the photographer, alluding to the body shot required of all aspiring models; I sheepishly explained that I do not engage in formal exercise. Fortunately, the stylist said that he would put me in a wet T-shirt, the illusion of bodily definition to be created through an admixture of wetness and drapery. We also discussed a method for creating nonexistent musculature: burying your fists under your crossed arms, you widen your biceps by pushing up against them with your knuckles.

As to clothing for the shoot—a large number of couturiers' names were invoked; it was promptly decided that I was "*not* Dolce and Gabbana." (It would later turn out that I was, however, Versace, Comme des Garçons, and Fruit of the Loom.) And as to my light brown, somewhat Amish haircut—"Don't take this wrong," the stylist said plainly, "but your hair is, it's . . . *mousey*"—it was promptly decided that I would be moussed.

=

In an attempt to effect gauntness and hollows, I ate as little as possible during the next two days. The day before the shoot, I ate, in order, a Triscuit, a Triscuit, two rice cakes, an apple, a Triscuit, and three rice cakes. But then at ten-thirty P.M. I had a collapse of will and rapidly ingested two bowls of Sugar Pops served in heavy cream.

In my hunger-produced delirium, I began to fear what the modish photographer-stylist team from the East Village might do with me photographically. My mind fixated on two possible tableaux: 1) I am in my underpants; 2) A tall, naked black man is coating me with honey.

At eight A.M. the following morning, I arrived at the photographer's apartment/studio, a location whose keynotes were Donna Summer and vacuuming. We proceeded to shoot for thirteen hours, both indoors and out, creating a variety of looks—young executive, soulful outdoorsman, clubby hipster, shaving yuppie, and something that the stylist called a "little-boy grungy look" (for which they provided a pregnant model to play my hippie girlfriend). In one outdoor segment I was asked to plunge down a set of

stairs some thirty-five times while maintaining an efferves-
cent smile—a feat that bordered on stuntwork.

The last forty minutes of the shoot were devoted to the
wet T-shirt shot. Having been instructed to take a shower
with the T-shirt on, I then wrapped a towel around my
waist and proceeded to crawl along the floor while the
photographer and his two assistants (also on the floor) used
a plant mister to spray me repeatedly and liberally with
water. I felt like a vine.

At the beginning of each segment, the photographer
would coax me, "Okay, gimme some looks," but the only
expressions that seemed to come naturally were utter hilar-
ity and, increasingly, mild irritation. After ten or so hours,
my powers of adorability began to wane. When, during the
young-executive portion of the shoot, a cat walked into the
frame of the picture, the photographer told me to "work
the cat." The cat wisely fled.

=

When I had made prints of fifteen of the shots, I next went
to Devron Technologies, Inc., to make comp-cards—the
postcards, bearing my phone number, measurements, and
a composite of several of the photographs, that I would mail
or give to agencies. A young male Devronite encouraged
me to put the wet-body shot on the front of the card and
the shaving and the outdoor shot on the back. I then asked
for his advice on the name change I was contemplating,
showing him a piece of paper on which I had written the

possibilities: Dack, Ruff, Spitz, Testostero, Henry Slade, Hank Maelstrom, and Odor Johnson.

"That part I can't really help you with," he said, forgoing the opportunity to launch the career of male model Odor Johnson.

I chose the name Henry Slade, evocative as it is of danger and sexual annihilation.

Forty-eight hours later I had my comp-cards and the twelve best photographs (now placed in a slick, state-of-the-art portfolio) in hand.

Most modeling agencies ask that prospective clients either mail them pictures or attend an open call at prescribed hours; I mailed off my comp-card to twenty-nine agencies, personalizing many of the cards with notes aimed at charming the receptionists and assistants who open the mail—"I'm posed for action!," "I'd be a model client!" I also sent Polaroids of my legs and feet to Parts, the agency that represents hand, hair, leg, and foot models; I appended these, "Leg's work together soon!"

I received four calls right away: two agencies wanted to set up appointments, and two wanted me to mail them more pictures. Given that most beginning models freelance with four or five agencies, I decided to cast a wide net; I went and visited twenty-six agencies in all, sometimes going at specified open-call hours, other times simply showing up and leaving behind a comp-card. "I'm a new face on the market," I would say innocently, waifishly, to the receptionist. "I was wondering if I could show someone my book."

"No dear," responded the harried, sixties-ish reception-ist wearing a pink cardigan at Ford Models. "They'll look at your card and call you if they're interested." I skulked out of the Ford lobby. But then several days later, a Ford booker with a heavy foreign accent left a thanks-but-no-thanks message on my machine: "You don't have the look we're going for right now." At first, I did nothing, amazed that the only agency that took the time to phone rejections was also the most prestigious one. But gradually curiosity and desire began to gnaw at me; I called her back and asked her to look at my book. "It won't help," she said. "I know what we sell." I asked again, explaining how the vogue for real-looking models made me think this might be my golden moment; she responded, "They want a stronger 'character look.' " I asked yet again; she said, "It won't help. . . . You have a good look, but it's not what's selling now."

Indeed, my weak character looks weren't selling at the larger agencies and the agencies that didn't specialize in commercial work (advertising used to promote products instead of haute couture). At Thompson Model and Talent Management I waited for about five minutes with a male bodybuilder and two top-heavy women—it appeared to be Large Breast Day at the Thompson offices—whereupon a booker sniffed at me, "You're not right for me."

"Am I too . . . real?" I asked.

"Or something," he replied.

A booker at the oddly placid Maxx Men spoke the words that soon enough became the refrain of my foray into the world of fashion modeling: "You're a little . . . *small* for us," she said.

"I'm six feet," I said.

"Are you?" she asked dubiously.

"I'm *just* six feet."

"Really? You don't look it."

"I come off small in person," I explained. "But I photograph very big."

But my efforts were to no avail. Agency after agency told me I was not tall enough; I started to feel extravagantly, resoundingly wee. When the booker at Thompson became the third person in one day to assert the theme of Lilliputia, I displayed my hands to him and tried to promote myself as a hand model. There are two types of hand models—glamor (hands must be virtually poreless and have long, tapered fingers) and product (hands are more athletic looking). It had occurred to me that I might qualify in the latter category. However, the booker sitting next to the booker I had been talking to said, "Darling, your hands aren't nice enough for hand work. Look at your nails—they're *painful*." When she told me to wave my right hand in the air, I did; she said, "Your look is very veiny." Then: "No, I am *not* encouraging you to work with your hands."

=

Not charactery enough, not tall enough, not veinless enough: my feelings of inadequacy metastasized into desperation. One day, having been told by a fashion industry insider that the people who run the male modeling agencies are "nightpeople," I put on a black leather jacket and black jeans and visited Omar's Men, a high-profile agency run by a hip Panamanian man named Omar. Standing in the agency's entrance I beheld a blur of cappuccino, stubble, and telephone terrorism. I walked up to a booker with shoulder-length hair and an earring; I told him that I wanted to show my book to Omar. "I can tell you right off the bat that you should go to a commercial agency," he said. So I told him, "I was talking to Matt Dillon at Café Tabac"—referring to a person I have never met, a trendy place I have never been—"and he said that I should talk to Omar."

"Well, we have a great men's department."

But no introduction to the great Omar was offered. I explained that every recent ad I had seen had used unglamorous, real-looking models: the booker responded, "That's what people are using now. But you'd do better at a commercial agency, I'm telling you."

So I went to commercial agencies. Two of them wanted me to pay them to include my picture on the poster featuring pictures of their clients—a fairly certain sign of an agency's low position in the agency food chain. At the first of these, located in Times Square, the Broadway Danny Rose–ish proprietor was literally yelling "Fuck the friendship!" into the phone when I entered. This did not bode well. At the second, located high up in the Empire State Building, the manic head of the men's division had tips for me: "You'll have to cover your blemishes with makeup when you go out on interviews," and, "Wear a Western boot with a heel." The prospect of running around Manhattan in cowboy boots and makeup was unexciting to me.

Two more legitimate-seeming agencies were equally enthusiastic. "You're a young doctor. . . . You're Dr. Kildare," an intense, vulpine booker at Formation told me. He was particularly excited about the shaving picture ("Fabulous. That's right out of an ad. That *is* an ad"). When he told me, "With your looks, your teeth, your respectability, I'd be really surprised if you weren't making thirty to forty thousand dollars a year in a year or two."

When I visited the boyish, mid-twenties booker at Foster-Fell who had called me after my mailing, the first thing he said to me was, "I've got a job for you" (what he actually meant was that he had a go-see—an audition—for a sportswear catalogue for me). In our frantic ninety-second-long exchange, during which he took two phone calls, he gave me the address of the go-see and described the desired look as, variously, "preppy gone bad," "sexy Ralph Lauren," "sexy preppy," and "preppy sexy." To be thusly described was highly flattering; although I did not get the job, it was an honor, as they say on the Oscars, to be nominated.

In the end, five agencies took two or more comp-cards from me and said that they would be "sending me out." It is with some hesitation that I report that, of these five, the one with which I felt most comfortable was an outfit called FunnyFace. "Tell me about the name FunnyFace," I said to one of the bookers. "This doesn't have anything to do with . . . *clowns*, does it?"

"Clowns?" he asked. "No."

"You don't represent circus clowns?"

The booker calmly assured me that the agency had nothing to do with that segment of the entertainment community intent on scaring children.

=

Over the course of the next month I went out on two other go-sees—one for Newport cigarettes and one for Shields Shower Gel. The drill for these two go-sees, as for the sexy preppy one, was the same—I would show up, hand over a comp-card, scout the waiting area for paragons of beauty upon whom to feast my eyes, have my picture taken, and then leave. It was fun.

But I was still not working.

=

"Give them all thirty-two flashing! If you smile long enough at someone, they'll smile back. You have to believe. You *have* to believe in yourself," the man was exhorting a class of nine of us. He pointed at his torso and continued, *"This* is the temple of the living God. Let go and let God. God is the best actor-singer-dancer there is."

Yes, I had committed an act of fashion-model hubris: I had enrolled in an acting class. To wit, "How to Get into TV Commercials," as taught by former Grecian Formula spokesman Bob Collier.

My decision to position myself at the intersection of

hucksterism and thespian blather did not stem from a need to renounce the life of bookers and comp-cards; it was simply that this model wanted *to talk*.

Thus did I follow my initial class at Bob Collier's TV Studios and Theater with four private lessons with Mr. Collier himself. Sometimes breaking into snatches of show tunes in the middle of a conversation, other times stuffing his pockets with oversized facsimiles of one-thousand-dollar bills to make the point that commercials are lucrative, Mr. Collier, part showman, part evangelist, is an affable, silvery-maned gent with a voice that is redolent of product endorsement. Our private sessions were composed of equal parts on-camera training and discussion of the Science of Success, a program of positive thinking derived from Napoleon Hill's book, *The Master-Key to Riches*. As Mr. Collier repeatedly told me, "What the mind can conceive and believe, it can achieve."

"Here," Mr. Collier said in our first session, "I want you to have this." He handed me a Xeroxed sheet and explained that twice every day—on waking and before going to bed—I should read the affirmation printed thereon out loud. (We would both also intone the affirmation out loud during each of our sessions.) The affirmation:

DAY BY DAY IN EVERY WAY, BY THE GRACE OF GOD
I AM GETTING BETTER AND BETTER AND BETTER!

I AM HAPPY!
I AM HEALTHY!

I AM TERRIFIC!

I AM IMPORTANT!

I AM BEAUTIFUL!

I AM RICH!

I AM SUCCESSFUL!

I AM CONFIDENT!

I AM A STAR!

I AM HAVING A GREAT YEAR!

I AM FILMING MY FIRST COMMERCIAL BEFORE _____!

I AM MAKING BIG MONEY IN COMMERCIALS

RIGHT NOW!

"Remember that 'I am' is the name of the God presence within you," Mr. Collier told me.

During our sessions, he encouraged me to read Napoleon Hill's book three times, explaining, "Commercials are about happiness. And that's why I'm trying to change your head by having you read the book. Because if you're not happy, how can you sell happiness?"

=

I did not chant the affirmation when I wasn't in class. I approached the on-camera portion of my tutorials with ready amounts of vigor, applying myself to the zestful blarney of ads for Rice Chex and Mitchum deodorant and Ivory soap and Band-Aid Clear Tape, but I began to feel that my ambivalence about the fundamentals of positive thinking was keeping me from truly *delivering*.

"You have to love the camera and the camera will love

you back," Mr. Collier encouraged me one day. "Give it a name if you want."

"I'd like to call it Barbra," I said.

"Then call it Barbra."

This seemed to help.

I had no disagreement in principle with the Science of Success's main tenets: Make up your mind as to exactly what you want, have a burning desire, be willing to give up other things in order to get it. What was disconcerting was the conclusions that it led to. "That's why countries who have homeless people, who have crime, who have problems—this is why they have problems," Mr. Collier told me one day. "[The countries] haven't taught them that everything they need is right in here," he said, pointing at his head.

This troubled me; people are poor for reasons other than their inability to form mental pictures of cash in large denominations.

The Science of Success also had an awkward-making interpersonal aspect in its promotion of high expectations. Mr. Collier started our second class by saying to me, "I'm feeling happy, healthy, and terrific. How are *you* feeling, Henry?"

"I'm feeling . . . well, pretty terrific," I mumbled. At the beginning of the third class, he asked, "What's your good news?"

"Oh, I don't know," I said, looking at the floor. When, at the beginning of the fourth class, Mr. Collier asked, "What's your good news?" I suddenly felt I needed to testify, as if I needed to offer up some kind of remuneration for his assiduous efforts and quite genuine charm. I proceeded to tell a white lie by explaining to Mr. Collier that, minutes before coming to class, I had splashed on some new cologne and was feeling "rather terrific" as a result.

He looked at me with slight suspicion. Then he walked closer, leaned over toward me, and took a sniff of my chest.

"It's very subtle," he said.

During our last class, Mr. Collier led us on a forty-minute-long conversation about the state of the world and various media cover-ups of the last thirty years. My teacher, it came as little surprise, was a conspiracy theorist: he avowed that E. Howard Hunt had been on the grassy knoll in Dallas and that AIDS was a vaccine formulated by the National Institutes of Health and disseminated by Citibank-financed bloodmobiles.

When our conversation had coughed to a stop in the manner of an overworked burro on the edge of the Grand Canyon, we both found ourselves shaking our heads as we stared at the floor. After a long pause, Mr. Collier finally said, "What can we do about all this?"

"I don't know," I said. "But I don't think it involves commercials."

=

Indeed, after five classes at the Collier studios, the world of television commercials held increasingly less appeal for me. I was progressing well in my studies—having taped the Rice Chex spot several times, I could see my performance shap-

ing up into a thing of beauty, nuanced and rich with sub-
text—and yet it seemed that something was missing.

I realized what it was. In directing my attention to the
small screen, I had unintentionally renounced the thrill of
the greasepaint, the roar of the crowd, the dizzying splendor of so many thousands of theater clichés.

I had lost touch with my *craft;* I wasn't being asked to
make *choices.*

So, like the film star who returns to Broadway after a
too-long stint in Hollywood—granted, this star of stage
and screen had yet to actually *appear* on stage or screen—I
yearned to re-experience the magic of live performance. I
knew that following such a plan would limit the size of my
audience, would make it even more difficult to achieve
carved-in-granite immortality.

But I didn't care.

I would reach for the brass ring. I would firmly grasp it.
I would *hold on.*

And so I did what anyone in my position (no experience,
much enthusiasm) would do: I responded to an ad in
Backstage looking for volunteer hair models to work at a
Redken trade show, to be held at the Westchester Marriott.

=

On arrival at the appointed conference room at the Marriott—a throbbing nexus of haircare implementa and large-
hair-bearing women that instantly recalled a remote episode
involving an ill-tempered cocker spaniel and the Holiday
Inn at the Newark airport—I was handed two pieces of

paper by a wonderful, husky-voiced, red-haired woman named Wanda. One was a Xeroxed letter from Redken explaining that hair shows are held for the edification of professional hairdressers and that prospective models should not be dismayed if not chosen to participate. The other piece of paper was a form we volunteer hair models were expected to fill out; at one point, it asked which of the following I was interested in—haircut and style, hair color, permanent wave, hair pieces. Not sure how willing I needed to be in order to get hired, I put a check by the first and a question mark by all the others.

After I waited half an hour, the two male Redkenites who were walking around the room and talking to each of the models approached me. Both had clipboards. The hair stylist was blond and the colorist was brunet; for the purposes of this reportage, I will refer to them as Siegfried and Roy.

Roy said to Siegfried, "He'd be a good presentation model to escort the ladies."

Siegfried murmured in agreement. Peering around the side of my head and running his right hand through the side and back of my hair, Roy said, "Tell me where you're going with your shape."

I explained that I did not have a chosen trajectory for my shape.

"Remember that haircut you had when you came back from London?" he asked Siegfried. "That would be good."

Siegfried agreed. "Very short," he added. There was mention of some kind of encircling fringe.

"I had a color treatment that I thought would be fun,

too. If we left this long," Roy continued, tugging gently on my forelocks, "I could put in bolts of color underneath. You could swish them whether you wanted to see the bolts or not."

"This is sounding kind of elaborate," I said.

"It's not. It's easy to do," Roy assured me.

Siegfried moved the hair off my forehead with his hand. "This is where we'd see the bits of color?"

"Yeah," Roy said. "Actually, more like *hunks* of color."

Siegfried okayed the plan. He said to me, "It's going to be a really different shape."

"Like a rhombus?" I asked.

"I'm gonna build in a wall," he said, patting the back of my head. "And then we'll lose the wall."

Visions of men toting Sheetrock filled my head.

Roy, who had been writing notes on his clipboard, looked up. "We need a name for this," he said, squinting artistically at the proposed hunking area.

"That's your department," Siegfried responded.

Scribbling on his clipboard, Roy said, "Let's call it Peek-a-Locks."

=

Mine is a curious profession; trouble is my business. Traipsing from situation to situation—from vendor stand to civil service test, from bridal registry to bed and breakfast—I approach the unwitting world around me as a scientist his laboratory.

Occasionally, there is doubt. Often, there is guilt. Sometimes, there is the sensation that my already-ragged karma is being eaten at by cancer.

However, let it be said that at no point in my life did I ever experience this sensation more profoundly than while standing listening to these two men discuss the near future of my hair. My ordeal with Clifford at the dog-grooming certification test flashed before my eyes, as did the governor's seizure of my notepad. I was filled with a premonition that the world had come to avenge me and that the world had chosen the Westchester Marriott as the place for the showdown.

I thought: These two men are going to dye my head a violent shade of pomegranate. And then I will go home and my friends will call me Hairdo.

=

First Siegfried cut my hair. This went quite smoothly, and the resultant shape was quite flattering, even if the front was, as one of the other twelve models would later tell me, "a little bangy." I did not cavil at this banginess; and particularly heartening was the cut's lack of encircling fringe.

Looking at my newly created shape, Siegfried said to Roy, "You're gonna have fun with that."

"Yeah, I'm gonna have fun with it," Roy responded.

But moments later, Roy said to me, "I'm not sure I'll do the underbits. I want to concentrate on the overcolors."

"Overcolors?" I asked.

He explained that he was going to practice "unidirectional tinting" on me. "It'll look like a very strong sun is hitting your head from about this angle," he explained, holding his hand about a foot away from the top of my ear. "It's a sunburst effect."

"Will this be attractive?" I asked.

"It looks great," he said.

As it turned out, however, Roy did not have time to "do me" that day, and thus suggested that I return early the following day, the day of the show.

I did. I was not sure what my duties would be during the show; all I knew was that I was meant to wear the tuxedo that I had told Wanda I would bring.

Pandemonium reigned in the Redken conference rooms. As disco music blared from a tape deck, Siegfried and Roy and two other stylists beavered away on the various models. A Caucasian model in her early twenties who had been cosmetically and tonsorially Orientalized had four curly twigs snaking out of her head; the knee-length blond hair of another model was being painstakingly transformed into a ten-inch-tall fantasia of ringlets. A model who had missed registration the day before arrived; when she was told that she could be a wig model, she began to sob softly.

While reconnoitering to see whether there were any other male models (there was only one), I struck up a conversation with a twenty-something woman who appeared to be a friend and groupie of one of the models.

"Have you done this kind of thing before?" she asked.

"No," I said. "I mostly do lobe work."

"You mean for cars and stuff?"

"No," I explained, assuming she meant lube work, "ear-lobe work. I'm an earlobe model. Like for movie posters when it's a close-up of a head but the star has bad ears."

"Wow. Do you know Tom Cruise?" she asked.

"I did his *Top Gun* ones," I said. "For the poster, I mean."

"No sir," she looked astonished. "What's he like? He's totally short, right?"

"I don't get to meet the stars," I explained. "I just, you know, get a fax of their ears about a month before the shoot and then I train accordingly."

A vague look of horror came over her face; seconds later she ran off to join her friends in the bathroom.

Moments later Roy told me that I was to be a "tech model" and that he would do my hair on the stage. I said this was fine. I changed into my tuxedo and then waited for about an hour and a half to have makeup put on. During this, an anxious Siegfried entered the makeup room and made an announcement thanking all of us models for our time and wishing us good luck. "Without you," he said, "there is no show."

=

I still didn't know what my duties entailed. Then suddenly at about noon, eight of us models—some in formalwear, some in clubwear, all having had our hair partially or fully styled—were hustled downstairs and told to wait just out-side the threshold of the grand ballroom where the show was being held. When the doors were opened, we were told, we should file in past the audience of several hundred, turn to the right, and then strike poses of fabulousness and hauteur amongst the various product-laden booths the audience would soon be visiting.

A shudder of anxiety and excitement passed through the group. We could all sense it: our moment was approaching.

The doors were thrown open.

But something was wrong.

The audience had already gotten up from their seats. So instead of striding coolly before them for their inspection, we simply trudged with them over to the booths.

Indeed, even once at the booths, we models didn't seem to be so very exciting to the show's patrons.

"Do you know why I'm wearing a tuxedo?" I asked a woman in her forties who was looking at a photograph of an aerosol finishing mist called Spraye.

"Are you with the caterer?" she asked.

"No," I said. "I'm a model."

"With Spraye?" she asked.

"No, for my hair. I'm a hair model."

She looked uninterestedly at my coiffure.

"It's nice," she offered.

When I asked a second woman why she thought I was wearing a tuxedo, she said she didn't know, particularly given that the boy at the hotel's front desk was only wearing a blazer.

I was still not making modeling magic.

=

The show broke for lunch. At about one o'clock, the six-foot-long hoagie that would be the models' and the Redken employees' lunch arrived; Wanda took one look at it and reported, "Oooo—we're all gonna smell the same."

At two forty-five all of the models filed downstairs again and waited backstage. This would be the "tech" part of the show—that segment wherein Siegfried and Roy would, to a hammering disco soundtrack, perform the more elaborate and exciting cuts and dyeing processes onstage while on-looking members of the beauty community yelled, "Work it, Siegfried!," "Work it, Roy!" During this, the p.a. system broadcast the two men's detailed explanations of each cut; one of these ran, "We used a Brandy Mocha Java and then toned it down with Irish Creme on her highlights."

About a half an hour into the demonstration, one of the Redkenites tugged on my sleeve and said, "Okay—it's time." She led me to the side of the stage and, at the appropriate moment, pushed me gently forward.

My heart beat rapidly. Implicit in my anxiety was the fear that not only was I going to be transformed into a florid, high-butterfat cordial, but that hundreds of people would be watching this metamorphosis and, somehow, *learning* from it.

"It often seems to me that we don't take enough advantage of our male clients," Roy was saying as I sat down in the chair in front of me. "So Henry's a client who just walked into my salon and I'm going to turn this male client into a color client."

The following minute in time suggested to me that there

is indeed a God. Just as I looked to my left and saw Roy dip a small brush into the hair dye—a greasy, caramely goo that I eyeballed at one part hydrochloric acid, three parts Tia Maria—I heard Roy intone, "I'm going to do a process called Slights—slight highlights." Thereupon did he proceed to coat six radial clumps of my hair with the sweet-smelling unguent. No fringe, no hunks, no Peek-a-Locks. Just the sunburst clumps.

Minutes later, backstage again, I asked one of the Redkenites if I should wash the dye out of my hair. She assured me there was no need; but then, moments later, she walked up to me and said, "Yeah, you better run upstairs and wash it out."

=

When I looked in the mirror upstairs, the dye's effect was wholly unnoticeable. I rinsed my head under a faucet and went back downstairs. As I was turning a corner to go back toward the show, I said hello to the girl who had asked me if I knew Tom Cruise; she was walking the opposite direction with a friend.

"That's the guy," I heard the woman tell her friend when they thought they were out of earshot.

"Who?" the friend asked.

"The ear guy."

"Ewww," the friend made a sound of disgust.

=

There is a part of us all that longs to be immortal, that longs to have our every utterance and movement belong to the ages. Concurrent with this desire, however, is the realization that there are not enough magazine covers, not enough Senate seats, not enough medical breakthroughs for us all to make our names on. With this realization often comes readjustment, acquiescence.

I remember once talking to an actress who had been rehearsing a play under the guidance of a Svengali-like German director. The director had burdened the rehearsals with exercises, sensory work, and assorted workshoppy digressions.

"Do you think the play will turn out well?" I asked the actress.

"In a way, it doesn't matter," she told me.

"What do you mean?"

She sighed, a note of resignation betraying her outward perk. "Well, in the end," she said, "it's really about *process.*"

A hauntingly accurate description of my career as a male model.

WHAT IF THE ROYAL FAMILY WERE PUT ON THE ENDANGERED SPECIES LIST?

Monday   Aging sex symbol makes empassioned plea on Academy Awards for preservation of royals.

Tuesday   New commemorative stamp issued showing Queen Elizabeth II from four different angles.

Wednesday   Prince Charles and Lady Di are shot by tranquilizer darts and air-lifted to Balmoral, where they are encouraged to roam freely.

Thursday   World Wildlife Foundation issues bumper sticker: WARNING: I BRAKE FOR PRINCE WILLIAM.

Friday   Japanese maintain that harvesting of royal family by factory ship is actually beneficial to species.

Saturday   PBS airs documentary featuring extreme close-ups of Prince Charles perched on grass stalks.

Sunday   Team of naturalists circle in on bog in hope of flushing out Sovereign.

WHAT IF A TALENT AGENT UNDERWENT TIME TRAVEL?

1880 A.D. Agent sends troubled modeling client on go-see for Rodin's *Gates of Hell*.

1307 A.D. Agent tells the first victim of the bubonic plague that her life story is *"very* M.O.W."

2114 A.D. Agent visits space colony, calls cyborg leader "dollface."

88 B.C. Agent interrupts human sacrifice to ask competitor's Druid client, "Are you happy?"

1690 A.D. Agent confuses Huguenot with use of *package* as a verb.

WHAT IF JEAN-PAUL SARTRE HAD HAD A LITTLE IMAGINARY FRIEND NAMED SNEAKERS?

1942 Sartre scours Paris for a tiny beret.

1943 Sartre pens line, "Hell is other people"; abandons Sneakers in a cardboard box on the *métro*.

Afterlife of the Party

I t is the tendency of the urban resident, while waiting for his ship to come in, to fritter away his existence fantasizing about precisely how he will revel in that ship's exquisite cargo. In my own case, I have always maintained that chief among the advantages of possessing a truly lavish amount of money—besides the assurance that you would never again be forced to avail yourself of that food product that, when added to meat, makes *more* meat—is that such an existence would be the perfect basis for leaving behind a highly whimsical and elaborate will. A will that would make the distribution of moneys and personal effects an experience marked by agony and torment. A will whose dictates and codicils are so confusing that even county clerks would weep profusely.

Granted, the idea is less than gracious. It lacks charity and a fond indulgence for your survivors. However, consider this: When you die, a complicated will is the best way you have of dictating how often and with what intensity people think about you. It is the closest thing to legacy control that life has to offer. Your good deeds and interesting accomplishments are all very well, but once probate is over and the highboys and the Aubussons are dispersed to their new homes, who will attend to the eternal flame of your memory?

When I go, I want the searing anguish that only litigation can deliver. I want frayed nerves and sleeplessness and lots of intercontinental faxing. I want an otherwise meek descendant to call the executor of my estate and snarl, "Look, I just want you to know that if I don't bag the Chagall prints, my lawyers and I are *ready to mobilize.*"

=

When it comes to estate planning, I take all my cues from my grandmother. When she passed away, her heirs, eight of us, gathered to hear her will. It was written with the tenuous grasp of reality so common to those teetering on the brink of death, and so had exactly the note of vague caprice that I can only hope my own old age will engender. In it, after a fairly dry divvying up of dollars and real estate and securities, several of her more prized possessions were assigned in this fashion: "The Steinway grand . . . to a boy who plays," and "my Remington . . . to a girl who shoots." This set off a torrent of confusion—in the first instance because all five men present felt eligible for the piano, given that it was for a boy who *plays,* not a boy who plays *well;*

in the second instance because none of the women—all three of them working mothers living in the suburbs—could imagine a lifestyle that would plausibly accommodate either big game or skeet.

And then came the catalog. Several weeks after our first meeting, the bank acting as executor sent each of the survivors a booklet in which all of my grandmother's possessions not mentioned in the will were described and appraised—catalog-style—for our purchasing purposes. We could either receive one eighth of the combined value of everything in the catalog or could use that same money to buy individual items. The demotion from "heir" to "home shopper" was devastating; soon, however, we got into the spirit of the thing, and then in no time at all we were giving full vent to the more unattractive, bargain-hunting aspects of our personalities. We talked *merchandise*. We talked *items*. We talked—as a lawyer had advised us to—*intangibles*.

But then when it came time to actually go to Connecticut for the weekend and lay our claims at my grandmother's house—now a veritable yard sale of death—our consumerist impulses rammed head on with the distaste of having to even *touch* this lovely woman's memory-laden possessions, let alone buy them. This clash of opposing emotions led to a sort of grinding, manic anxiety; by the end of the first day, one family member's face was so swollen from crying that she looked like she had been boiled.

And then I realized that the catalog itself was only heightening the absurdity and confusion of the situation. The sniffy young appraiser had written it in the exaggerated and

ironical fashion of a man who resented my grandmother's
house for falling short of the Winter Palace. His prose style
found him alternately lost in a hazy revery ("one bifurcated
settee on ball and claw *pieds* . . . nineteenth-century English") and mocking with utter disdain ("one oversized
papier-mâché pig . . . *probably Mexican*").

=

And so we came to fan the flames of our devotion to our
dearly departed. We suffered over her loss, and we suffered
over her possessions. Thereupon did I realize that there is
another way to make the living tremble before a power from
beyond the grave. I speak, of course, of the inappropriate
bequest. A bequest of such unsuitability and incompatibility
that your heirs are left scratching their heads and muttering,
"What could cousin Eustacia have *possibly* been thinking?"

So when I opened *The New York Times* one chill March
morning and saw an advertisement for free appraisal days at
the auction house Christie's East (just below the detail of
an etching of a human eye, presumably reproduced from
currency, was written "Are you looking $10,000 right in
the eye?"), I heard the golden bells of opportunity peal.
Hying myself to 219 East Sixty-seventh Street on the appointed Sunday, I walked to the end of a line of some
eighty-five people on the sidewalk. As I walked, I noticed
that many people had paintings—most of which were
wrapped in bedsheets or blankets; one man had decided not
to cover his Renoir reproduction but rather to hold it in the

thirty-three-degree air by the wire on the painting's frame. Indeed, after I further inspected others' possessions, my insecurity about the value of my own humble offerings was somewhat buoyed: the couple in front of me were banking on a wall hanging, wrought in mirror and black and pink Plexiglas, of a woman wearing a large, stylish hat; the German woman behind me clutched a screw lock that she had bought at a junk shop on Long Island.

"It's medieval," she said to a man standing behind her who looked at her dubiously. "I'm sure of it."

The general tenor of the crowd was summed up by a man ahead of me in line who, pulling a porcelain figurine out of the cardboard box he was holding, said, "Oh, I'd love to unload this baby today."

When fifty minutes later a group of about twenty-five of us was allowed to enter the building, I was ushered to a card table behind which sat a woman in her twenties with a look of mild distaste. Draped around her neck were tiny pearls; her hair's drooping bow suggested that a large black velvet butterfly had perished on her head. She asked what I was going to have appraised; seeing that she was giving each person a piece of felt in a color corresponding to the category of his possessions (Paintings, Books and Manuscripts, Jewelry, etc.), I told her, "Collectibles." Awarded a piece of felt, I was told to wait upstairs on the third floor.

When my name was called out fifteen minutes later, I was directed toward the Collectibles table, behind which sat two well-groomed, clean-shaven men in their thirties. I put down the three boxes in which I had stored my treasures.

"My aunt sent me with this stuff," I said.

"You don't look too happy about it," one of the men said.

"Well, I don't really know too much about collectibles," I offered. Then, handing over the small metal box into which I had put a bag of copper grommets bought at a hardware store for $2.39—the kind you might see at the edges of a tarp or rain poncho—I said, "This is Uncle Buzz's grommet collection." The two men peered into the box diagnostically. The right eyebrow of the man holding the box twitched; the other man's face took on a slightly suspicious cast.

"Do you know how old they are?" the one holding the box asked.

"I'm not sure. He didn't make them. He collected them. I think they might be pretty old."

He sighed. "Well, all we can really do is take Polaroids of them and maybe refer you to someone."

With that, the other man stood, and walked off with the grommets.

I next produced a wallet-size cardboard box in which I had put a house key, two pieces of chalk, a pebble, a garlic husk, and a lot of pencil shavings. The outside of the box bore a label reading, DES CHOSES INCONNUES.

"These are some things we had lying around," I said.

The man looked at these items. He shook the box lightly, causing the husk to ruffle.

He moved on to the next box.

This third box contained a shard of a chicken bone that I had dried out in my oven.

"That's a bone fragment," I said. "It's from Mrs. Filth-Winterbottom's ulna."

The man's face betrayed no emotion.

"These aren't the kinds of things we handle," he said. "What you might do, though," he continued as he took one of the pieces of paper stacked on his right, "is get in touch with Nostalgia."

On the form—a list of fourteen auction houses and galleries—he made an X next to a Long Island concern called Nostalgia Galleries. I folded this piece of paper and put it into my pocket.

"They might be interested in this kind of thing," he concluded.

"In . . . household items?" I asked.

"Yes. And they'll have themes. One week it might be stained glass, another week furniture."

"Or it might be bone fragments," I added.

"I'm not sure about that one," he smiled tightly.

"It's very old," I offered. "She was pretty famous. She was the electricity heiress."

"Oh, really?" he said, trying to remain affable. "Well, you can ask them and see. See, in our department, we mostly specialize in things like movie posters, animation, movie cels—things like that."

When the second gentleman returned seconds later, his

sour expression suggested that, having subjected the grommets to his Polaroid, he was now less impressed with them than he had been before. Handing me the box of grommets, he said, "We can get in touch with Nostalgia and see if they're interested in these."

I thanked him heartily and left. As I took the subway home, I realized that the two men had issued conflicting directives—the first had suggested that I contact Nostalgia; the second suggested I wait for Christie's to contact Nostalgia. Not sure which course of action to pursue, I chose the latter, as it was more flattering to my ancestry.

=

When I had heard nothing two months later, I called the Collectibles department at Christie's East. The man who answered the phone sounded startlingly like the first appraiser.

"Hi," I said. "I came in two months ago on a Sunday when people came in with things from their house? I just wondered if you'd heard something."

"What was the piece you brought in?" he asked.

"It was a collection of grommets. It was Uncle Buzz's grommet collection."

"Yes, I think we told you at that time that that wasn't something we would handle here."

"Oh . . ."

"I think we made that clear when we gave you the referral sheet."

"Oh, right. It's just that you took three Polaroids of

them. I thought maybe they were, well . . . somehow *special.*"

The man reiterated his stance; I thanked him and hung up.

=

When I discovered that the number listed on the sheet for Nostalgia was disconnected, I called the Collectibles department again and was given the name of one of Nostalgia's partners, whom I will call Ed Winston. "They split up," the Christie's employee told me, "but essentially it's the same situation as before."

Over the course of three phone conversations with Mr. Winston, I suggested four days when I would be able to drive out to Long Island and show him "some things that my grandmother left me," but our busy schedules prohibited our convening.

"What kind of stuff are we talking about?" he asked during our first conversation. "Are they toys? Are they statues?" During our third conversation he asked, "Are they Hummels? Are they porcelain? Is it Disney, is it Deco?" Each time I responded that I wasn't sure what the objects were, saying simply that they were collectibles and that I would ask my aunt to explain their significance to me.

Finally, I followed his suggestion that I send him Polaroids. Two days after I had mailed them, on a Saturday at four-thirty P.M., a rather incredulous Mr. Winston called me.

"So what's the story with these pictures?" he asked.

"Well, it's stuff my grandmother left me," I explained.

"Right, but what about these descriptions?"

"My aunt explained those to me. She provided them."

"You're telling me," Mr. Winston said, reading the label that I had affixed to the back of the Polaroid of the grommets, "that 'these hollow, copper-backed grommels were collected by Uncle Buzz, the popular children's entertainer of the thirties and forties,' and that 'he was indicted in 1948'?"

"They're not grommels," I said, hoping that this misunderstanding lay at the root of Mr. Winston's seeming skepticism. "They're grommets."

"Big difference," he said. *"Who's Uncle Buzz?"*

"He was an entertainer. He performed at society parties. I wasn't really familiar with him either. My aunt told me about him."

"Why would anyone want these? And you're telling me—" (At this point he read portions of the label I had affixed to the ulna Polaroid.)

This bone fragment is from Eleanor Filth-Winterbottom's ulna. She was, as you probably know, the eccentric British heiress who was an intimate of both Rupert Lavish and Neuralgia Crest.

She was considered to be a great beauty (although Grandmother always disdainfully referred to her as La Poitrine); she lived on a boat on the Thames during the twenties called *A Boat on the Thames During the Twenties*. She died of a skiing accident in Gstaad in 1972; she built up a lot of speed on the last stretch and then skiied *right* through the lodge.

Although cremated, she asked that her ulna be pre-
served and divided amongst her heirs.

"And you're telling me," Mr. Winston was saying, "that
this bone fragment belonged to someone named *Eleanor
Filth-Winterbottom*?"

"Yes. The heiress."

"Who is Rupert Lavish? Is that a real person?"

"He was a poet."

"You sure you don't mean Rupert Brooke?"

"He wasn't as famous as Rupert Brooke. Look," I
pointed out, "these people may not *still* be famous, but
they were quite well known in their day."

"*Neuralgia Crest?*" he said, laughing. "What is that?
That means, that means 'a pain in the ass'!" He started to
laugh.

"And nothing on the *choses*?" I asked.

He started to read the *choses'* label: "These whatno—,"
but he started to laugh uncontrollably. And then, suddenly,
there was a thud and a crash—it seems that he had collapsed
with laughter.

For the record, the *choses'* label:

These whatnots came from my grandmother's desk. A
noted court stenographer and author, she wrote the
1954 pamphlet "The Contemporary Felon: Whither
Diction?"

The husks in the photo allude to Grandmother's
fascination with garlic.

"I'm sorry," he said when he got back on the line. "I don't mean to make fun of your—"

"No, no, that's okay," I said. "I realize that parts of this may seem comical."

"Yeah, a little," he said.

"So, so you're sort of saying that these things have no value?" I asked.

"I don't know *anyone* who would want this stuff," he gasped, letting loose another round of laughter.

=

The city cannot accommodate all of our hopes and aspirations; there are times when it seems to exist only to steamroll our uniqueness.

Three months before my grandmother passed away, she asked me one day to take her to a doctor's appointment in Hartford. After her session with the doctor, she shuffled out to the receptionist's area, where the harried receptionist gave her another appointment for a date two months later. My grandmother, given, at this stage in her life, to black humor and dire pronouncements, looked at the appointment date and said, "Oh . . . I'm not sure I'll even be *around* then," whereupon the receptionist, clearly missing the point, chimed in, "Well, if you can't make it, *just call.*"

And this, I suppose, is the prerogative of the deceased. For once we are no longer in this life, we will no longer be free to engage in fine dining with the objects of our affections. We will no longer be available to sprawl on the hot tar roof of our building, wallowing as the cool breezes of summer curl up tendril-like against our socklessness. We will no longer be able to walk into the atrium of a skyscraper, marvel at its accumulation of chrome panel and plashing fountain and smoky glass divider, and conclude that we have entered the depths of an enormous scotch and soda.

No, we may no longer be able to revel in any of the beguilements and enchantments that brought us to the city in the first place.

But we can always call.